By this you will know

As the coldest winter blows

And when nothing can burn

It is then you must return

Trek the Jessap Waters

Seek for the dust of the Father

Dump the dust in the water's foam

It is then you will be welcomed home

The Legend of the Wood

John C. Mehl

authorHOUSE®

AuthorHouse™
1663 Liberty Drive, Suite 200
Bloomington, IN 47403
www.authorhouse.com
Phone: 1-800-839-8640

First published by AuthorHouse 10/22/08

ISBN: 978-1-4343-8109-5 (sc)

Edited by: Kiersten Mehl

Printed in the United States of America
Bloomington, Indiana

This book is printed on acid-free paper.

To my love and inspiration, K

Chapter One

Λ ϝireside Sτoꞅy

Sometimes a story tends to repeat itself. Maybe it is told with different characters, in different lands, and with different challenges or battles to overcome. In that way, this story is not so different. Except that this story is different to me. That is because this story still lives on within me with great affect on who I am and how I live. It is not my story, but one that was told to me some time ago by an old man who has now passed on. But I will not go on about how this tale came to me, for if I did you would likely not believe me. Not yet anyway.

It began, as most do, in relatively peaceful times. There were no significant battles being fought, save the occasional dispute between certain men and countries who strive for more wealth and power. Yet far away from the chaotic cities and fast-paced lives of their citizens was a softer and warmer sort of existence. Rather than buildings and walls growing higher and higher, here the growth remained primarily in the tall trees, and the speed pertained to the rushing rivers. The vast majority of the inhabitants of this land were solitary, un-tame and wild. This was the young and magical land we now call "The West."

This land did not have a specific name in those times, for men had not yet recognized its worth nor desired its treasures. That is not, however, to say that there were no people living there. Great people, powerful and ambitious men and women called this great land home. No, they were not those we call 'Indians,' for this is even before their time in the land. These people were more like explorers that had found their place to settle down and live their lives. There were very few of them, that is roughly thirty or so, and they were generally able to live harmoniously with each other and with the nature surrounding them.

There was not one central leader of the group, but four families that each had a representative to speak for them when rare pressing matters arose. Each family had its own personality and skill, which is probably why they stayed so tightly bound. One family, led by the aged and strong Essiah, was particularly skilled in gathering food off the land. Next were the builders, a family led by the young Skoar, who contributed different forms of shelter and protection from the weather or the occasional hungry bear or mountain lion. Then there was the family blessed with knowledge of all sorts of practical uses for the plants and animals, led by the wise Horrico, who, though aged, looked younger and stronger every time you saw him. Perssa, the lone female leader of the families, came to be head of her family after the recent unusually bad winter led to the death of her husband. As her family made up the greatest portion of people, Perssa always made herself

3

and her family available for whatever task needed assistance, and they could always be counted on as a sort of overseeing or coordinating presence.

The final head of the group was actually not part of a family, but was one man named Blakely. The old, bright-eyed man would likely be the head of the entire group if he so desired such a position. The respect and admiration that he commanded was unparalleled to that of anyone else in the group. Quite possibly the reason for all of his popularity was the role he played within the group. He was the storyteller, the song-singer, the 'entertainer' so to say. Blakely was the only member of the group that was around for what he called the 'old times,' the days in which the group had just begun to settle in the land. In addition to his tales of tradition and history, Blakely would also tell wonderful stories of heroes and goblins, epic battles, and silly little tunes.

Blakely could be counted on at a moments notice to reminisce on these classic, sometimes terrifying or humorous, tales and tunes. As he would walk through the forest, build new shelters, or wait for the fish to bite, Blakely was always more than willing to share the stories and songs of the 'old times.' However, Blakely's best treasures, the very greatest stories and tunes, could only be heard on one very particular night. Every night in which there was completely no moon, Blakely would light up a large fire and let the stories and rhymes flow. Due to this exact specification and considering how treasured Blakely's fireside stories were, every single man, woman and child was sure to be in attendance on these nights.

And it just so happens that our story begins on one of those very special nights when Blakely began by saying, "If you would all come a little closer please, tonight I will tell you the tale of the heroic *Battle of the Southern Meadow*."

Sustained excitement seeped up from the camp like the smoke of the fire as the people drew closer and closer to Blakely until some were almost sitting on

5

his lap. Blakely sat in a very eager manner against a tall, overhanging pine tree. He was a truly regal sight to see with his full head of pure white hair gleaming in the firelight and all dressed up in his usual buffalo skins and leather moccasins. There was a remarkable contrast of colors, as seen in the light of the flames, with Blakely's glowing white hair and the dull color of the animal skins he wore in comparison to the rose red color drawn out in his cheeks by the extreme cold. His ability to captivate the people, more than his mere appearance, was what any eye looking upon the scene would notice.

As Blakely began telling this tale, occasionally pausing either for dramatic effect or to take a puff from his pipe, the people were mesmerized with every crisp and clear word he spoke; they hardly noticed the beauty surrounding them on this moonless and cloudless night. By how close and bright the stars appeared, one might have thought they too gathered around to hear the great tale. A soft, yet brisk westerly breeze blew just enough that the trees swayed in a slow and steady manner, as if to set the rhythm for the occasional tune within the story. In fact, tonight, as on every night the group gathered to hear Blakely's stories, it seemed as if the entire world was yearning to hear every word of the tales and tunes.

Not far from the fire there were numerous empty dwellings that glowed with the dim light of torches. Due to the skill that Skoar and his family possessed, these dwellings were built sturdy, large, and warm. Their four corner posts were made from some of the biggest trees in the forest. Between those posts ran various animal furs, not for decoration, but rather to trap the warmth inside. The roofs slanted slightly backwards and contained a small shaft that stuck up for the smoke of the entry fire to escape. On either side of the doorway hung two torches that illuminated the small area in front of each home. This area, largely considered to be the most important and certainly most used part of each home, was always busy with different activities and decorations, except, of course, on nights like this. Every single one of these 'front grounds,' as they were called, had some kind of seating–whether made of stumps, old logs, or unique small stools created by members of the Skoar family.

"And at that moment, just when all looked bleak and over for Jessap and his men, a bright light shot across the sky," continued Blakely.

Upon glancing at the awestruck and silent crowd around him, one might have thought that Blakely's very words held their own lives in the balance.

"Jessap grasped onto all the strength he had left and rose to his feet. The very clouds seemed as if they turned into ash as this strange light rushed across the sky. Jessap followed it all the way down to where the evil Goc and his force were waiting on the edge of the meadow. The violence with which the light met the army caused such a roar that its echo remained for what seemed like an eternity. And after the dust had settled, the only remnant left from Goc's entire force was his own bloodthirsty sword, lying singed in the weeds."

With that last word, Blakely leaned back against the tree he was sitting under and drew an extra long puff from his pipe, as if to tell the crowd that he was finished with his masterpiece. Not a word was uttered amongst the crowd for some time, as many had finally begun to notice the magical night that surrounded them and were very satisfied with simply taking it all in. After some time passed, the beautiful silence was broken by a small voice.

"Blakely, sir," whispered Jeran, a grandson of the Skoar family. Jeran–not yet a man, but older than the other children of the group–had the appearance of an energetic boy on the verge of becoming a young man. He had curly brown hair, bright green eyes and carried himself in a respectful, yet excitable manner.

Jeran had found his way through the crowd and up behind the tree upon which Blakely was resting. So his whisper, though soft and quiet, still gave Blakely a little start.

"Yes, young man, what is it?" Blakely asked. "Although before you answer, I might remind you to be cautious of startling old boys like me in the future. You never know what I might do to you out of fright," Blakely said with a twinkle in his eye.

"Well, I was just wondering, what was the light?"

"Ahhh, that is a very good question boy. Let me answer that by asking you this: Do you believe that there are things in this realm that cannot easily be explained?"

As he was replying to the boy, many others, both young and old, were leaning in, for the curious light was on their mind as well.

"Cannot be explained?" asked Jeran, noticeably confused.

"By that I mean things that are not normal, things that we may not see or hear of often, if ever at all."

"Oh yes, sir!" exclaimed Jeran. "I know there are big bears around, though I have never seen one."

"Right you are, right you are," chuckled Blakely. "And this light is, in that way, a lot like the bear. It is very special and very powerful, and so we should give it respect. But the light, young one, is different from the bear because it does not roam these parts. In fact," he whispered, drawing the boy very close, "it is not even of this realm."

"Not of this realm?!" interrupted one of those who was intently listening to the conversation. "What do you mean by 'realm?' How can anything in this land be not of this realm? Is it another wood then?"

"Well, young lady, let me put it this way," replied Blakely, turning towards the woman who had somewhat sharply asked the question.

11

It was Hurell, granddaughter of Horrico, who was sitting not far from Jeran on the opposite side of Blakely. Blakely said 'young lady,' not because she was a child (for she was in fact older than young Jeran, but still much younger than Blakely himself), but because her tone seemed somewhat disrespectful.

"Simply because you may have never experienced certain things," Blakely continued, "does not necessarily mean that they do not exist. What if there were places you could not get to, even if you walked forever? Why shouldn't there be another realm? Why shouldn't there be a thousand realms?"

"A thousand realms?!" exclaimed Jeran with great excitement. "Really?"

"Now, now," said Blakely, turning back towards the young boy and patting him on the arm. "Let's not get carried away with ourselves. I never said there were a thousand realms. I simply was trying to make a point to those who apparently became a part of our nice little conversation without our knowing it.

But let us not travel too far from our original topic. You still don't know *what* the light actually was. Now remember, what happened to Goc's sword?"

"It was burnt?" Jeran said, quite unsure of his answer.

"Right you are. Which means that the light, in one way or another, must have been partially made of…" Blakely said, leaving the end open for the boy to finish.

"Fire!"

"Precisely! The light was partly made of fire," Blakely said, getting great joy out of the young boy's logic.

"But don't we have fire in this wood? What was so special about that fire?" Hurell interrupted again.

"Young Hurell," Blakely said patiently, turning once again to the woman. "First, remember the light was not necessarily only made of fire, but only partially. Secondly, there need not be anything special about the light itself, except why it struck such a place at such a time."

At this point the crowd, with the exception of Hurell and Jeran, was again observing in an awestruck and silent manner. The fire had long since died because with all the attention back on Blakely, no one had tended to it. As a result, the light, with no moon, was very dim.

"Was someone helping Jessap and his men?" asked Jeran.

"Someone, yes! Someone indeed!" remarked Blakely, almost dropping his pipe from the excitement. Blakely repositioned himself, as he became aware of the fact that his words needed to be heard by all. "You see, when Jessap was discovered that day on the bank of the river, no one ever asked him where he came from. Of course they were not as curious as some are about those things," he said, grinning. "And Jessap never brought up the issue due to Goc's immediate invasion."

"Then Jessap was from... somewhere else! And his people sent the light to destroy Goc!" erupted Jeran.

"Mmmm...You could say that, young one, and you would be right near the truth of it all. But enough of this prolonged tale for tonight. It has become impossible now for my old eyes to see, and I need some young and sharp eyes to help me up and lead me home. What about it, Jeran, my wise young lad?"

Jeran looked quickly back at his father who nodded in approval, and he helped the old Blakely to his feet and handed him his famous cane. The cane was easily recognized because it must have been the straightest stick in the entire mountain range. Mounted on top was a small, remarkably smooth rock that Blakely could always be caught staring at and fidgeting with. The rest of the crowd slowly started to break away and head back to their warm homes.

Without a doubt, every mind lingered on the strange new addition to the *Battle of the Southern*

15

Meadow–every mind including that of young Jeran as he walked across Blakely's front grounds, holding the old man's arm. But Jeran knew he dared not bring up the issue once again; the time for fire tales was over, and Blakely was noticeably exhausted and ready to be in his warm home. That is why he was so surprised when Blakely turned to him and said, "Now that we are alone and can return to our old conversation, why don't you take a seat on that stump right there."

After Blakely told Jeran to take a seat, he went inside and was there just long enough to give Jeran enough time to take in the situation. He looked around the front grounds, at the seating and Blakely's torches, noticing how everything was showing signs of age. The stumps and logs appeared utterly exhausted from being used on countless nights when company would stop by Blakely's grounds for some warm cider and friendly conversation. The surrounding trees were scarred with strange marks and carvings, the aftermath of Blakely's younger years and many wooden hatchet-throwing competitions. Even with the light of the torch, the smoke-shaft at the top of the home disappeared into the darkness because it was so completely covered in dark ash.

"This must be the oldest home in the whole wood," Jeran said, unaware it was aloud.

"The oldest that is still standing; that is true," replied Blakely, who had just appeared through his entryway with a couple of animal skins in one hand and a newly restored pipe in his other. He smiled at the embarrassed reaction of the boy and replied by giving him a small, but warm bearskin. Sitting down and re-lighting his pipe, Blakely said, "Now where were we? Ah, yes, Jessap and his 'people,' as you said it."

"They are people, aren't they?"

"Now, Jeran, listen carefully," Blakely said, trying to choose his words wisely. "As I said before, there are things in this world that cannot easily be explained, things that are almost never seen. If we are to ever understand these things, it takes a little effort on our part. This is similar to the fact that you understand the idea of a large bear even though you have not yet encountered one."

"But I've seen big bear tracks and big bear... droppings," he said with a slight giggle.

"Indeed!" Blakely responded excitedly. "You have seen what the bear has left behind. You have seen what the bear has done. Therefore, you understand the bear. It is that same way with Jessap and his... 'people.' They have acted in our land; they have left tracks behind."

"Like the light!" yelled Jeran, jumping to his feet. But he quickly sat down when he noticed the stern look Blakely gave him, reminding him not to disturb the sleeping wood. "Like the light?" he said in a softer voice.

"Yes, the light was a manner of protection for Jessap. For you see, Jessap knew all too well the depth of Goc's power and for whom he fought. But that is another story."

As the two were talking, they did not get the chance to look up and notice that the bright stars in the sky could no longer be seen. Instead thick clouds had rolled in and were now stealing any warmth remaining in the air. They started to reveal their silent approach by sending a sharp frozen breeze with a few snowflakes that fell on the bearskins of the young boy and the old storyteller. At first sight of the flakes, Blakely's eyes seemed to light up with joyful tears, and he said, "Young Jeran, I believe that is all the discussion we can afford tonight. Now you must head back home and get a good night's rest."

"Rest? How can I rest with all this new stuff I know?"

"I'm sure you'll find it easier than you think. Now keep that old bearskin wrapped tightly around your chest, and do not wander."

The small boy rose with a sort of contented disappointment, if that could make sense. He knew he must go, but this had been the most exciting and rewarding night of his young years. Before he turned to walk off of Blakely's front grounds, he paused. Looking back and catching Blakely's fond gaze, Jeran knew that they shared the same feelings. He quickly gave Blakely a warm and firm embrace then skipped and frolicked toward the darkness of the forest, and past that to the torches of his own home that could faintly be seen in the distance. Right before he disappeared into the night, he turned his head once more, just in time to see the familiar sight of Blakely fidgeting with the stone on top off his cane as he entered his home.

Chapter Two

Strangers In The Wood

Several days later, most of the other families were able to move past their utter fascination with Blakely's story and the inevitable questions. It still made for great conversation as people went on with their daily routines. Some of the older members of the families thought Blakely was simply trying to explain complicated ideas, such as where the weather comes from, which meant they were at least a little less curious. Others did not know what to make of Blakely's post-tale discussion, so they tried to pretend as if the story ended with the singed sword. No one, however young or old, was naïve and unintelligent enough to even wonder whether or not Blakely had simply made it up on his own. They knew Blakely too well to think that. No story Blakely told was ever doubted, even the strangest of the strange. All anyone had to do was watch the old storyteller as he spoke and see the emotion and resolve in his eyes to know that these tales were real to him.

The younger children constantly prodded Blakely for more stories and more answers, to which he was more than willing to give. In fact, upon looking at the activity of the families in the most general way, nothing had changed in the wood at all. The family of Essiah was still either out hunting or feverishly gathering food off the land before the brunt of winter rolled in. Horrico and his own were busy preparing their combinations of plants and minerals to protect everyone from disease and any sicknesses that may come with the cold. The Skoar family was working harder than most because they knew, after the last winter, the people would need stronger and warmer dwellings. Because of this, most of Perssa's family was lending their services to this effort.

It was not surprising to anyone that Jeran volunteered to work on Blakely's home when assignments were handed out, and no one with a kind heart, seeing the desire on the boy's face, could turn him down. Blakely and Jeran had many conversations during those days, yet strangely none of them had anything to do with the story of Jessap. On the contrary, they were mostly on the topic of Jeran's own family members. Blakely was very interested in what Jeran thought of them, even though he knew them well himself.

"Oh, I know young Grandor," Blakely would say. "But I do not know him as well as his family might. You see, Jeran, people tend to reveal their true identity without any disguise when they are only dealing with their family. If they are kind to their family, then they are, more likely than not, a kind person. If they are humble around their family, then no doubt they are truly humble."

"I wonder what my family thinks of me," muttered Jeran softly, seemingly worried.

"Jeran," replied Blakely, who had apparently stopped calling him 'young,' "do you remember the story in which Helleh was teaching her son a lesson about accepting oneself as imperfect before judging others? The very song she sang to him might be sung to you.

> *Mistakes and missteps, failures and flaws*
> *Infects the large and the small*
> *Yet, he who sees his own wrongs*
> *Is the wisest of us all.*

"I can tell you this much, Jeran," Blakely continued. "You have been given the opportunity to look into the depths of others and speak on what you see. But instead, first you realized that you might have some faults yourself. That at least tells me you are no fool."

Of course Blakely's vote of confidence brightened up young Jeran, and thus, he was ready and willing to answer any questions Blakely might have. Their conversation went on throughout the day and into the night, with Blakely asking more questions pertaining to certain members of the families.

Meanwhile, on the outskirts of the wood, Dalleo, son of Essiah, was patiently tracking a large buck. Presently, he was quickly trudging through the mild creek that marked the boundary of the wood. The last piece of evidence Dalleo had found suggested that the buck was about to cross the water and head down into the meadow. Dalleo knew, even though he wanted to maintain a safe distance so as not to be heard, that he must cross the creek and reach the meadow soon or else risk losing the trail.

25

Hatchet in hand, Dalleo would be a frightening surprise for any man or beast. His solid figure, weapons for the hunt adorned over his body, and arms and legs that were as firm and strong as the trunks of oak trees made Dalleo intimidating enough for any man. Yet it was his face that would be his most intimidating feature. His sharp, sculpted cheeks and stone dark eyes reflected his own steadfast and strong character. His long, midnight black hair covered his face, as if to conceal and shield the face of a beastly man. He towered over any other son of Essiah and was by far the strongest and thickest man of all of the families. That being said, he was remarkably competent in controlling his large frame as he stealthily crept through the forest.

As he approached the meadow, he paused to take a short drink and control his breath. He kneeled behind a large evergreen tree, making sure to keep every move as silent as possible. Taking a long drink, he closed his eyes and tried to calm his nerves. The importance of calming oneself and being in control of all motions is magnified when hunting with a wooden hatchet. In order to be effective with the hatchet, Dalleo would need to be within only a few steps of the buck. Evidently, this required extraordinary patience and skill, and even the best hunters were usually unsuccessful.

Dalleo opened his eyes and rose to continue his pursuit. He steadily descended on the meadow then paused behind the last few groups of shrubs. The buck, apparently unaware of its predator's presence, was sharpening his great antlers on a nearby aspen. This was a tremendous break for Dalleo; the scraping antlers would drown out the sound of any small mistake in movement that he might make. Dalleo crouched down and moved across the shrub line until he was behind the buck. Breathing steadily, he visualized his intended path to his prey. Unfortunately, there was a pile of dead branches in his path that would surely give up the intruder's presence before he was close enough to strike.

Just as Dalleo was trying to decide on a new path, he suddenly noticed the buck had stopped his scraping and was scanning the opposite side of the meadow. Dalleo dared not to move and risk drawing the buck's attention. His task required a good seven or eight more unnoticed strides, which relied on the distracting noise of the antlers. The buck appeared very nervous as he raised his head and pricked his ears forward, attempting to pick up any scent or subtle noise. Yet no sooner had it raised its head than its body fell lifeless to the ground after a deafening crack echoed through the trees and a small plume of smoke rose from the brush across the meadow.

Dalleo stared in utter shock at the motionless buck, as blood seeped from a small wound high on its neck. However, that shock was outdone still by the next sound Dalleo heard; laughter and shouting came from the trees, and he could make out the quick footsteps of two approaching men. Dalleo stayed crouched and hidden by the shrubs, trying to gather his thoughts and make some sense of the last few moments. As he remained hidden, two men appeared out of the trees from where the explosion came. Both men were still laughing and talking very loudly as they approached the fallen buck. They wore large hats with feathers sticking out of the side and heavy leathery skins draped over their shoulders. One was waving a long, thick shaft in his hand as he marched forward.

Outsiders in the wood were a rare occasion. In fact, the only living member among the families who had actually seen another person outside of the wood was old Blakely. The men he had encountered were two shipwrecked sailors who had made a long journey in search of help. He found them terribly injured after a vicious bear attack; they did not make it through the season. These men whom Dalleo encountered were definitely not injured, nor did they appear lost. All of their commotion stopped instantaneously when Dalleo decided it was time to stand and face these unfamiliar men.

At his emergence, the look on their faces was most definitely one of great surprise and confusion. One of the men shouted something at Dalleo and crouched down, as the other nervously fumbled the long tool in his hand.

Despite being immensely confused by the men and their reactions, Dalleo started slowly walking towards them, trying to determine who they were and figure out what tool the man was fidgeting with.

"Stay there, you!" screamed the crouched man in a nervous, yet loud voice.

"You are not from these parts," replied Dalleo in his deep, strong voice. "Who are you?"

"Don't-t-t move. We don't want any t-t-trouble," stuttered the other, who had stopped fidgeting with the shaft and now was pointing it in Dalleo's direction.

"Who are you?" Dalleo repeated more sternly, not fearing the threats of the two men. "And what did you do to this animal?"

By this time, Dalleo was only a short stone's throw from the men, and he could now make out their facial expressions. He could see that both were terrified and shaking violently, which seemed to give him a little more confidence. Dalleo stopped to look at the dead buck at his feet. He saw a deep, circular wound that had a little burnt hair surrounding the hole.

Suddenly, Dalleo heard quick footsteps approaching from behind. He whipped around to see his brothers, Dilen and Drake, running toward the meadow. No doubt they came in response to the loud crack, as they were hunting in the area as well. Much like Dalleo, these two young men were of great size, yet noticeably less fearsome in stature and appearance than their older brother. For one thing, their hair color was much lighter, almost yellow, and cut much shorter, hanging only to the bottom of their ears. Their etched faces bore a definite resemblance to Dalleo's, yet they had brighter eyes.

They froze as they reached the edge of the meadow and saw Dalleo standing at bay from the two strange men. The brothers slowly approached Dalleo, shooting confused looks between the men and their brother.

"Dal," said Dilen. "What is going on? Who are these men?"

"All of you, stop where you are!" yelled one of the men. "Don't come any closer!"

Dalleo, after getting the attention of his brothers, nodded toward the dead animal. One bent down and closely inspected the wound with his hand.

"Some kind of burning rock killed this buck," he said, hesitantly inspecting the area of the wound.

"We do not know you men and do not need to continue in fear. If you are for peace, tell us who you are," Dalleo said very calmly. Yet hidden by the shrubs, he clutched his wooden hatchet hard in his hand.

The two men whispered quietly to each other, but both kept their eyes directly on the three brothers.

"We are peaceful men," said the one who was rising from his crouched position. "No trouble here."

He began to approach the brothers slowly and unthreateningly, but the other remained behind, still holding the shaft.

Drake caught Dalleo's attention and hinted with his eyes that they should attack with their hatchets, but Dalleo shook his head.

"Speak quickly," Dalleo said. "Who are you and what are you doing here?

"We are men of Spain. I am Señor Mediche, and this," he said, motioning for the other man, "is Señor Oroso." The other man hesitantly lowered his shaft and walked toward the brothers.

"Spain... is that your father? Your family?" Drake asked the man, as all five were now close to each other, encircling the fallen buck.

"Spain is our home, our land. And we have been sent to travel these lands and see what they have to offer," Señor Mediche said with more confidence now.

Generally, when Mediche or Oroso encountered strangers in unfamiliar lands, they had to speak slowly. However, they could see that Dalleo and his brothers spoke well. While they showed some confusion, they still understood what Mediche was saying.

"You are a traveler then?" Dalleo asked.

"Sí, travelers, señor," Oroso added, trying to become part of the conversation.

"And what is that shaft in your hand?" Dalleo asked, now turning to Oroso. "Is that what killed this buck here?"

"Sí! This," Oroso said, showing his weapon, "is our masterpiece, Mediche's and mine."

Oroso was apparently very proud of this weapon, but also very protective of it. Dalleo tried to take a closer look, but Oroso quickly retracted it and put it into a long, narrow pouch. With the strange and intriguing weapon put away, both of Dalleo's brothers moved in a little closer to get another look at the wound on the neck of the buck.

"Well, now we have told you who we are. Who are you? How many are you? What are you doing here?" Mediche said, scanning the trees for any more unsuspected men.

"I am Dalleo, son of Essiah, and these are my brothers, Dilen and Drake. Our families have lived here off of this land for as long as our father has been alive. We belong to a group of families that lives in the wood not too far from here. We are all the sons, daughters and grandchildren of those four families; led by Horrico, Perssa, Skoar, and our father, Essiah."

"Ahhhh… You are natives of this land. Most likely never ventured out beyond the mountain range," Oroso said rather arrogantly. "Might we, Mediche and I, pay a visit to your people? No doubt there is much we could learn from each other."

The brothers looked at one another, unsure who was going to bear the burden of answering this question. There were no stated responsibilities when it came to such uncommon circumstances, so they were left wondering how they should respond.

Noticing their obvious hesitancy, Mediche chimed in, "We are no threat to you and your people; I assure you. We are only two men traveling through these lands with the intent of reporting back to our king."

"And your weapon," Dalleo said, turning to Oroso, "that is no threat either?"

"No, señor." Oroso replied, "You see, it takes quite a long time…"

"Not a threat at all," Mediche interrupted.

This abrupt reply increased the brothers' curiosity and they became a little more concerned with the unusual men and their weapon.

But at long last, Dalleo finally said, "So be it. We will speak with our people and may allow you to accompany us back to the wood. However, for now,

I will stay here with you as my brothers return home with news of our meeting."

"Fair enough," Mediche replied.

With that, Dalleo turned to his brothers and walked away from the men.

"You must tell father of this. If he rejects their visitation, gather at least five other men and quickly return to tell me before I bring them across the creek."

"Dal, do you think they are dangerous?" asked Drake.

"Dangerous, yes. But without a doubt, if we have numbers on them, even their weapon could not defend them. I noticed 'Orso,' or whatever his name is, struggling with it when I first showed myself. Yet with that in mind, make sure to tell Blakely of their weapon, for he may know something more of it. Now go quickly."

With that, the two brothers rushed up through the trees and disappeared. Dalleo turned around and went back to the men, who had turned their attention to the buck and were preparing to clean it.

"Dalleo, isn't it?" Mediche asked, rising to his feet. "We were thinking this buck might make a perfect gift to you and your people if you would accept it. We are only two and do not need as much food as this, and it might possibly ease your worries about us."

"Thank you for your offer. But we are more than capable of supplying our own food."

On this point, Dalleo was speaking the truth; the family of Essiah was never short on food. However, Dalleo mentioned nothing of his unsettled worries of the two men.

Just about the time that Mediche and Oroso had killed the buck, Blakely had just left his front grounds and headed toward the Jessap Waters. These waters were named after the great Jessap, for it was here that he was originally found lying on a rock just above the rushing water's edge. Blakely slowly trudged through the damp wood, whistling loudly as he went. His tune was so loud and joyful that it seemed to awaken the entire wood as he approached. The birds echoed his tune as they darted from tree to tree, seeming to follow old Blakely. The Jessap Waters were not far, yet Blakely seemed to have packed enough supplies to last for days into his large blanket that he wrapped up and threw over his shoulder. Of course in his other hand, guiding and supporting his way, was his well-known cane.

He had not traveled two hundred paces and he could already hear the distant roar of the swift water, even over his carefree tune. Blakely took a deep breath and sighed aloud. Flashing an even bigger smile, he quickened his pace. In what seemed to be only moments, Blakely could finally make out the white, foamy water, bubbling over the rocks. If someone had been walking beside Blakely as his feet hit the rocky beach, they might have been able to hear him reciting something with bright, beaming eyes.

"…It is then you must return," Blakely said, intentionally half-shouting in order to hear his own words over the water.

"…Trek the Jessap wa…" Blakely abruptly stopped his recitation as a crashing thud sounded from upstream. As Blakely quickly stumbled out farther onto the rocks to catch a glimpse of what might have made the startling noise, he could faintly make out an enormous, dark figure crashing toward him over the rocks and rapids.

The object was still too far for Blakely's old eyes to see clearly, yet the expression upon his face revealed that he was not nearly as startled as he had been moments ago. As the object rushed closer to Blakely, he could finally see that his assumption was correct; the object was a large tree. It had apparently fallen from the higher forest, shoved over by the weight of the fresh snow and heavy winds that were normal in the higher land. It was also obvious that this tree had traveled quite a distance, for all of its limbs had been violently ripped off and the trunk bore many scars from protruding rocks that lie in its way. To Blakely, this was yet another sign that the cold and fierce winter had arrived.

Blakely watched as the huge trunk tumbled by and continued down river. He sat down on a nearby stone and tried to light his pipe, yet no spark would come from his firestick. He tried several more times and then laughed aloud saying, "How foolish I am. There will be no chance for fire this winter. Not *this* winter…" He leaned back on a large boulder quite near to the water's edge and watched the rushing water as if he were watching a show.

"Blakely!" yelled Sharai, a beautiful young woman from the Perssa family. She came pushing trees and bushes to the side, still dressed in her long and light apron. Even the mess of her afternoon sorting of the fruit and her obvious rush had not diminished her stunning appearance. Her smooth, brown hair flowed over her shoulders, and she had green eyes that typically sparkled like light reflecting off water. However, at this moment her eyes were not sparkling, but instead had an alarming sharpness to them.

The rushing water drowned out her sudden approach, and her call to Blakely made him jump. Blakely quickly turned around to see Sharai running toward him with frightened, wide eyes.

"Two men…with Dalleo…at the meadow," Sharai stammered while gasping for air.

"Two men? With Dalleo?" Blakely gasped, trying to make his way to Sharai as he stumbled over the loose rocks. "What did they look like? Is Dalleo safe?"

"I think he is safe. Dilen and Drake were with him and just sent me to find you."

"Come, we must return," he said. With that, Blakely emptied out his pipe, grabbed his cane, and scurried back into the trees toward the wood.

In a surprisingly short time, Sharai had led Blakely to the place where she had last spoken with the two brothers. At first sight of Sharai and then Blakely, Dilen and Drake ran toward them and frantically started to explain their encounter all at once.

"Steady, young sons of Essiah. One at a time," Blakely said.

"We, Dilen and I, were out trying to track a buck when we heard a loud crack from the meadow!" Drake explained with great excitement. "We immediately took off toward the noise. When we reached the meadow, we found Dal standing there with two men we had never seen before. They looked very nervous, and one held a long shaft of some sort that hurled a fiery rock and killed the buck."

"A fiery rock?" Sharai asked. "How strange! But Dalleo is alright?"

"Yes," Drake replied. "He stayed with the men when we left to get help. From the looks of it, the

43

men seemed weary of him. Father is out in the forest searching for herbs, so we sent for you."

"One can never be too careful when there are unknown men with unfamiliar weapons," said Blakely. "But nevertheless, we will meet with Dalleo and come to understand who these men are and why they have come. Let us move."

With that, they all quickly rushed off toward the meadow. Dilen and Drake led the way while Sharai assisted the old Blakely, whose body was showing signs of strain from all the hurry.

When they arrived at the meadow, Dalleo was again examining the wound of the dead buck. Mediche and Oroso were off in the distance sharing a drink from their flask. At first sight of Blakely, Dalleo quickly rose to his feet to meet the group.

"Dalleo, are you alright?" Sharai asked anxiously.

"I am fine. But, Blakely, I do not trust these men. Their whisperings and secrets reveal the fact that there is more to them than we can see."

Blakely nodded and stepped forward as Mediche and Oroso now approached.

"Ah, you must be this fine man's companions or family. I am Señor Mediche of Spain, and this is Señor Oroso," Mediche said with a low bow, and Oroso did the same.

Both parties studied each other as the introductions were presented. Seeing the men for the first time, Sharai's eyes were drawn to the Spaniards' large hats and bright feathers that stuck out of the sides. Blakely noticed the skins the men wore around their shoulders; the leather was not smooth and worn as Blakely's used and weathered skin, but it was rough and unevenly cut. The hair on the faces of the men also attracted much interest; it was cut neatly and had evidently taken some time and care to design.

After the introductions ended, Blakely spoke up and said, "Do you men have a camp near here, or are you passing through?"

"Well, both, señor. We have been on this range for several days now and are trying to seek out a more permanent shelter to wait out the winter," Oroso said.

"And how is it you came to this range?" Blakely asked.

"An assignment. We were to explore these lands to discover what adventures and type of men reside here," Oroso answered, again revealing his willingness to speak the first thoughts that come to mind.

"And how long has your journey lasted?" Dalleo asked Oroso, trying to take advantage of his loose tongue.

"Oh, roughly three months or so," Mediche said, trying to redirect the questions his way once more. "And how long have you been here?"

"For as long as we have lived," Sharai said, unaware of the sharpness with which she said it.

Blakely gave her a quick look of caution and then replied, "Our people have lived here for some time without seeing many unfamiliar men. You must forgive our... unfamiliarity with new men."

"Absolutely, señor," Mediche said, bowing. "There is no offense, for we are on your grounds."

As the conversation continued, two questions crept into each of their minds: How was this meeting to end, and were these men welcome to come to the wood?

Fortunately, Mediche eased those concerns by saying, "Well, it is getting dark, and Señor Oroso and I must be getting back to our camp. If it pleases you men and your beautiful young lady, we would like to return to see you again tomorrow. Maybe then we can meet the rest of your people?"

"We will discuss the matter amongst ourselves," Blakely replied very frankly. "But we will meet you here tomorrow around mid-day."

To this Mediche and Oroso agreed, not that they had much of a choice, and walked across the meadow to retrieve the fallen buck.

As the two men picked up their prize and walked away, Dalleo turned to Blakely and said, "Blakely, I'm sorry, but I do not trust these men. They have secrets that they are not sharing with us. They always choose their words too carefully."

"I agree, Dalleo. Though we would also be wise to often watch our own words and how we say them," Blakely said, giving a quick glance to Sharai. "Yet we must address this issue with the family heads. Dilen and Drake, you two will spread the word to Essiah, Skoar, Horrico, and Perssa that we are to gather tomorrow morning at the fire pit before we come here to meet the men. Now, let us return."

With that, Blakely cast one last long gaze across the meadow and walked back toward the wood. Dilen and Drake followed him, chattering amongst themselves, while Sharai and Dalleo stayed back. As the chatter of the brothers faded away, Sharai turned to Dalleo with a concerned look in her eyes.

"Dalleo, what is going on? These men frighten me."

"I know, my love," Dalleo said, grabbing her hand and holding her close. "They are only two men. Even with their tricks and secrets, they can be no real threat."

"But I don't fear their force or their power. I fear the dishonesty in their eyes."

Dalleo gave her a soft kiss on her forehead and slowly walked back into the meadow. His silence showed that his focus was elsewhere. He stood there until the unmistakable feeling of falling snowflakes broke his concentration.

"The storm has come," he said, looking up at the darkening sky. "We should catch up to the others. Do not be so concerned."

"Dalleo, it's not just the men."

"What else then? The storm? Don't tell me you're afraid of the snow." Dalleo said with a slight laugh.

"Dalleo…" Sharai said, grabbing his hand as he walked past. She stared at Dalleo in such a way that he knew this conversation was far from over.

"What is it?"

"There is something else, something… wonderful."

All of a sudden both of their moods changed drastically. Sharai went from expressing obvious fear and hesitation to eagerness and expectation. Dalleo, on the other hand, had been distracted, but now was focused on what Sharai had to say.

"Horrico gave me the news from his final tests today. We are going to have a boy! I have already told both of our parents and families and was going to tell you after you returned, but so much…"

"HA!!!" Dalleo said, lifting Sharai up off of her feet and spinning her around. "Our child is going to be a boy! We're going to have a boy!"

With intense emotions running through them, the couple was speechless except for many stammering words of disbelief. The persistent excitement of the past few hours overwhelmed Dalleo, and he could not hold back the tears any longer. Because these tears were such a rare sight coming from Dalleo, upon seeing them, Sharai could not hold her own tears back. They both relished in this moment for some time with laughter and tears until the severe cold and new snowfall forced their celebration to calm. Dalleo tightly draped his skins around Sharai, taking great care to bundle her up completely. They both turned and trampled through the thickening snow back toward their home.

Chapter Three

In The Hall With The King

Once back at his front grounds, Blakely sat covered up in his great grizzly bear skin and rubbed the smooth rock on the end of his cane. Even though the snow was falling very steadily now in large flakes and there was no chance of lighting a warm fire, Blakely had no intention of going inside. This day had brought so many thoughts to his mind; he would not be able to lie down without sorting them out.

'These men were strange indeed, strange and secretive. Had they really simply stumbled upon us, or were they looking for us? Should they be allowed to come back to the wood? Would it be possible at this point to sufficiently protect and hide these people should the men have evil intentions? And what of this coming winter? Are those chosen to make the journey acceptable choices? Ashtar and Andros would surely desire to embark on such a journey. But what of Dalleo, Sharai, and their coming child? They may be hesitant to make the voyage with the baby either on the way or recently born. In any matter, there is no question that this winter is the sign the king told me to expect. There is no mistaking it now.'

Blakely brought his cane close to his old eyes and squinted as he could only faintly make out the words he knew so well. The words were written in a strange, straight-edged manner. The letters had no curve to them and were printed in a reflective silver color that had all but completely faded through the many years Blakely had carried it. But no matter, Blakely held the words deep within his heart by now:

> *By this you will know*
>
> *As the coldest winter blows*
>
> *And when nothing can burn*
>
> *It is then you must return*
>
> *Trek the Jessap Waters*
>
> *Seek for the dust of the Father*
>
> *Dump the dust in the water's foam*
>
> *It is then you will be welcomed home*

Blakely softly rubbed his fingers across the inscription and asked, "How long has it been, O' King, since we last spoke in the Great Hall of Jerudan?"

With this thought, Blakely's mind traveled back in time to that moment when he stood in the hall with the great King Jariel.

This majestic hall held beauty that can only be described with the best of words, and it was well known to any person throughout its realm. However, the people of the wood did not know of it, because the wood existed in a land far outside of this realm.

Within this realm, lie the land that the great Jessap, the great King Jariel, and the great Blakely hailed from. Jerudan, the greatest city of that land, was situated at the convergence of two mighty rivers. Jerudan was not built upon common soil, but on a massive and remarkably smooth rock of land. The city itself consisted of an intimidating stone wall that surrounded several large collections of dwellings, which included the royal citadel towering over everything in sight.

It was inside this citadel that the Great Hall of Jerudan resided. In accordance with the surrounding aspects of Jerudan, the hall was awe-inspiring. It was adorned with only the finest and most valuable decorations and designs. In its entryway hung a magnificent silver chandelier that sparkled with all sorts of diamonds, rubies and other gems. The door itself consisted of two large stone wheels that would roll back and forth to open and shut the way to the hall. An inscription above the door was printed in the same straight-edged manner as the writing on Blakely's cane. It read:

Enter The Great Hall Of Jerudan Friend Or Foe; Friends May Stay And Prosper, And Enemies Will Surrender And Go.

Upon entering the hall, one would notice an immediate brightness regardless of the amount of sunlight shining into the room. Brilliant colors emanated from the various decorations, tapestries and designs illustrated on the walls. The tapestries that draped from the ceiling were collected as gifts from surrounding allies. Their depictions ranged from realistic portrayals of the great city to colorful, undefined patterns and shapes. The designs on the walls were all alike. Each wall between the giant windows displayed the symbol of the entire kingdom of Jerudan; a large boulder standing strong between two crashing walls of water.

Numerous tables and chairs were set throughout the hall for the occasional ball or feast. The head table, for royalty and honored guests, was positioned at the front. Beyond the head table was the focus of the entire hall: the throne of the king. Standing taller than any living man, the throne was known as the most valuable asset in Jerudan. It was adorned with blue ambers and silver crystals and padded with a silky blue fabric.

It was upon this throne that King Jariel sat when he and Blakely had their conversation. That day, however, was not the usual joyous visit between the king and his young advisor, Blakely. Jerudan was under great threat by the demon army, led by Hershath, who was after the king's throne, both literally and figuratively. With his royal guard forming a perimeter around the hall and the deafening noise of the ensuing battle outside the walls of Jerudan, the king was desperately trying to charge Blakely with his orders.

"You must accompany my son, Jessap, to safety! There is no other choice!" the king had said.

"Yes, my king, but where? Hershath has cut off all paths of retreat." Blakely said, pointing to the map he had laid out before the king. "The demon army has surrounded the eastern and western shores, and we could not likely fight through them."

"There is no need to get to the shore, only the water."

"Sire?"

"The ashes!" Jariel exclaimed. "My father's ashes! If there be no place in this land where Jessap can be safe, then you shall go to another land entirely."

"What have your father's ashes to do with this?"

"My father's wise man, Correll, told me at my father's death that because he was not born in this land, the ashes of his body did not belong to this world. When combined with the common element of the two realms, they would return to their own realm, carrying along anything or anyone in contact with them."

"But, sire, should I then never return to Jerudan. For if that be the case, I would rather die here by the hands of Hershath himself."

"Correll told me that to return, the same method should work; the water being the common element."

"Should work? What if I have used up all the ashes upon my arrival?"

"Blakely, there is no time! Hershath is upon us, and I cannot spare my son, Jessap!"

"Apologies, sire. I was thinking too much with my head and forgot my place," Blakely said, bowing low and rolling up his map.

"Blakely," the king said softly, touching his shoulder, "you are the only one I trust with something so dear to me. Take care of him, and yourself."

"Sire," Blakely said with a slight smile, and he was off.

A sudden loud crash occurred. It took Blakely a few moments to discern if the crash occurred in his dream or if it had awakened him. Unfortunately it was the latter, and Blakely found himself disoriented and confused. He had realized now that he had fallen asleep on his front grounds and had dreamt of Jerudan. However, the dream was not now his chief concern; he needed to determine the source of the loud crash that woke him.

He tried to rise up from his resting place, but found his body extremely cold and stiff. He mustered up all the strength he had simply to ask, "Who is there?"

From inside his home came a sudden silence. No more noises of rummaging, only very faint whispers. Blakely strained with great difficulty to sit up and turn around toward his home. The only reason Blakely was able to see anything at all on this dark, fireless night was that the moon was still high in the sky dimly revealing the basic shape of the objects that surrounded him. Of course, he could not see into his home, but he heard whispers and knew someone was there.

"Who is it?!" Blakely called once again, now with much more strength than before. He was beginning to warm up inside his bearskin.

The whisperings stopped, and for a few moments there was absolute silence. Blakely was beginning to wonder whether this was some trick being played by young boys and girls who were simply afraid to get caught. It had never crossed his mind that there might be any wrongdoing, as such issues were very seldom in the wood. That is why, without fear, yet with great effort, Blakely rose up and entered his home.

At the entryway, Blakely paused and once more demanded a response. This time there came the soft rustling of someone standing up, and the prodding of a pair of footsteps headed toward Blakely. By the weight of the steps, he knew these did not belong to children. Thus he took a few stumbling steps back.

"Señor Blakely," said the voice. By the accent and word choice, there was no mistaking it now. The voice was that of Mediche, and most likely the second pair of footsteps belonged to his companion, Oroso. Blakely's face, if anyone would have been able to see it, turned from confusion and fear to great anger and resolve. He took a few steps forward into his home and firmly tapped his cane on the ground, as if to show the men that he had no fear and was now taking a stand against them.

"I do not know what business you men have going through my quarters. For that matter, I do not know why you would be here in the wood in the first place. But at any rate, you will explain yourselves clearly and without deceit."

"Señor Blakely, fullest and most humble apologies. However, I must admit that we are overcome with joy. For when we first happened upon your home and saw you lying with no movement in this extreme cold, we thought you dead."

"Do not merely flatter me, explain yourselves!" Blakely said, obviously impatient and seeing through the man's smooth words.

"When we returned to our camp after our encounter with you, we found four large cats rummaging through our camp and destroying it. So it is fortuitous that we happened upon your camp here, specifically your own home."

"Fortuitous indeed. Yet that does not explain why you are in my home now."

"Fire, señor," chimed in Oroso. "We were searching for some source of fire to try and warm you back to life."

"And you say you happened upon our camp and my own home, which is situated at the very end of our grounds. None of this is adding up. I have no more time or patience for your secrecy and lies. I will settle this matter."

With that, Blakely turned and began to walk back across his front grounds to gather several other members of the group to help detain and guard these treacherous men. However, he only made it a few steps when he was struck with a sudden blow in the back of his head and fell to the ground. His face hit the ground with a great thud, never to rise again. The great Blakely was dead.

Chapter Four

Λ 'Vile, Cursed Day'

The sun was straining in vain to break through the dense clouds and warm the frozen land of the wood. This lack of light resulted in a very dull and gray morning. The cold bit harshly, causing most of the people to remain in their warm, or at least warmer, homes. The few braving the cold were doing the most essential jobs: clearing the trails through the village, preparing the morning meal, and completing renovations to the dwellings for extra protection from the cold.

Dilen was one of these braving the cold. He had volunteered to help Skoar finish some last essential projects and was making some small repairs on the roofs of several homes. He was just tightening a knot between two branches when Drake interrupted his work.

"Say, Dilen, you been working on many homes already?"

"True, Drake. I'm trying to finish up before we go to meet those men. And you might help me out if you're not still too stupid from your sleep."

"Where you goin' next?"

"Over to the twins' place."

"Oh, well done then; send me all the way across the wood. All right, just a few extra layers to the top then?"

"That's right. Make sure to make your knots extra tight. Not like last time, when your handiwork almost brought down Dal's entire home."

"Right, it was one simple branch."

"Simple enough for you to handle."

"I'm done with you," Drake said, as he threw a snowball that hit Dilen right on his arm.

With a laugh, Drake turned and trudged through the thick snow back to the cleared trail that ran through the center of the wood. As he walked, he noticed the calm of the wood. There was an obvious silence this morning, an absence of chirping birds and cheerful greetings; the dreary light reflected this solemn sentiment. Even though the trail was clear, it still did not make for an easy walk. He avoided the difficulty of trekking through deep snow, but the uneven, icy snow made for slick and cautious travel.

When he reached the home of the twins, Drake called out in an intentionally obnoxious tone, "Good morning! I say, good morning!"

"What is it?" yelled a voice from inside the house, followed by the sound of footsteps.

Out came the smaller of the twins, Ashtar. He was wrapped up in heavy cloths, and his dark, disheveled hair stuck out every which way. The cloth over his head, as most in the wood wore to keep warm while they slept, was made of an extremely smooth and soft fabric. He was stretching his arms out as high and wide as he could, hitting one of his hands against the doorway.

The twins, with exception to their height, were remarkably identical in appearance and demeanor. As sons of Horrico, they were known for their adventurous spirits and the times they would go on excursions for several days to find rare herbal remedies. They were well liked among the families and were as close as two brothers could possibly be.

"What do you mean bothering us this morning?" asked Andros, joining the conversation.

"Dilen sent me to work on your roof. I can't say I'll be particularly quiet, though."

"Eh, do your work. We're just staying in to keep warm."

"Very well then. I'll gather the wood and be back in a while."

"Well if you don't even have the wood, why bother us?"

"Bad manners, I guess," Drake said, and he turned to go search the forest for the necessary branches. Unfortunately for Drake, there was no clear trail into the forest, so he had to make the tricky trip half climbing and half swimming through the waist-high snow.

He finally came to the beginning of the forest and last of the homes–Blakely's. Exhausted and starting to sweat, Drake knew he must rest for a moment to avoid catching a chill. As he lie back against a nearby tree to slow his breathing and bring his body back under control, he looked over toward Blakely's front grounds and saw the old man sitting out on his usual stump, covered up by his great bearskin.

"Little cold to be out just sittin' around, eh, Blakely?" Drake yelled to the old man. But no reply came back. In fact, there was no movement or reaction at all.

"Say, Blakely! Little cold isn't it?" Drake yelled again, thinking that his first attempt went unheard. There was still no reply or movement.

"Well then, he must be sleeping, which can't be good for the old man," Drake said to himself with a deep sigh.

He began to head toward Blakely's front grounds, which was only a stone's throw from where he was. As he got closer, he raised his head to call out again, but stopped every movement of his body. He could now see Blakely's face and could see that he was not sleeping, for his eyes were open and staring blankly upward. Noticing that Blakely's bearskin did not rise and fall with any breath, it was then that Drake came to the horrifying conclusion that Blakely was dead. Drake stared at this awful and surreal sight for what seemed like an eternity. When he could bear the pain in his heart no longer, he hastily retreated to the wood with frozen tears stuck to his face.

Making his way back through the thick snow was now even more difficult due to a severe decrease in strength. Drake's eyes could barely focus through flowing tears, and his unstable and shaking body prevented any significant progress. The terrifying image of Blakely's lifeless face refused to vacate his memory despite constant efforts to erase it. Running through his head were the questions of whom to notify first and how he would say it. How do you tell people that the greatest man anyone in the entire wood has ever known is dead? However, there was no room in Drake's head to focus on his deplorable task; the grief was too strong.

The vast mixture of emotions that cluttered Drake's mind caused him to be completely oblivious to Dilen's calls to him from the twins' front grounds.

"Drake!" yelled Dilen, standing on a large stone in order to make himself more visible. When this last attempt failed to draw Drake's attention, Dilen hopped down from the stone and trotted over toward Drake.

"Drake, you fool! What were you going to use to…" Dilen had just come close enough to Drake to see the anguish on his face. When his brother's eyes met his own, whatever tears Drake had been able to hold back now flowed freely, and he fell to the snow. Dilen stumbled through the snow and quickly arrived at his brother's side. He bent down next to Drake, laid his hand on his brother's trembling head, and waited for his brother to collect himself enough to speak.

After a long period of weeping and attempts to console, Drake was able to speak the dreaded words to his brother: "Blakely is dead."

Upon hearing those words uttered aloud, Drake broke down again, and Dilen was unable to speak, to move, even to breathe. There was not anything that either brother could say or do that would make this moment any easier to bear. So they sat there for some time, sharing tears and embracing each other. Dilen was the first to break the silence by asking, "How, dear brother? How did it happen?"

"I…I do not know," Drake said in broken words. "I just found him si… sitting there on his stump, eyes open and looking up."

"You think he was out there all night then, freezing in the cold?"

"Stop it! I don't want to talk about it! It's bad enough to see it in my mind without having to describe it."

Dilen knew his brother was right; it was simply his disbelief in the issue and his efforts to make some sense of what had taken place that forced out his questions. Finally, Dilen stood up and stared over toward Blakely's home, a sight he had almost been avoiding in order to escape the reality of his brother's words. But as he looked toward the front grounds and could faintly make out the area that he could always expect old Blakely to be sitting, the reality started to tear at Dilen's heart.

"We must go tell others; they have to know," he said amongst frozen tears.

Drake slowly rose up, completely weak and emotionally battered. He and his brother had to use each other as support to walk through the thick snow toward the cleared path. Stumbling along, they made their way in the general direction of the middle of the wood but had no real idea where they were going first, or for that matter, who they were going to tell.

As they came closer to the homes of the Skoar family, young Jeran came skipping out of his home, jumping into a snowdrift. Even with all their confusion and unsettled minds, they knew enough at that moment to protect this young man from being the first to hear the news. They went the long way around Jeran's home, which brought them right up alongside the homes of Perssa and her family. As they passed the last few Perssa homes, coming nearer to their own family's homes, they saw Dalleo and Sharai out on their front grounds, sitting bundled up and talking. That decided it for them; these two would be the first to know.

At first sight of Dilen and Drake, Dalleo saw that they were not their usual cheerful selves, and thus, he ran to them to see what the problem was. The frozen tears on their faces showed that something horribly awful was about to be revealed to him. He had not often seen such a look on the faces of his brothers, and he was not looking forward to the news he was about to hear.

"What is it, dear brothers? What has happened?" Dalleo asked, trying to look into their faces for some truth.

"The words are too painful to continue to utter, brother. And yet they must be said. Blakely has died," Drake muttered.

The pain of these words shot to Dalleo's head and heart simultaneously with a powerful sting. He stammered back and fell down into the snow with his muscular body trembling mightily. His tear-filled eyes rose to his brothers' eyes, looking for some kind of sign that it was some unforgivable and downright cruel lie.

But there would be no relief, as both brothers looked at him with eyes of great sorrow and suffering. No one was able to say anything for some time; the moments were simply cast away to despair. As Sharai came over to see what great evil could cause these three men to topple over in grief, Dalleo rose to take her aside and tell her the news. He wrapped his arms around her, whispered in her ear, and held her tight as she gave a sharp cry.

After many questions, countless tears, and statements of disbelief, Dalleo finally said, "We must tell the others before the day drags on. There are eyes that should not see the sight you saw, Drake, so I will go to the house and take the necessary actions with…" He could not finish this sentence, and no one in the group could bear it if he did.

"Shall I go to tell my mother?" Sharai asked, determined to get her mind focused on anything else.

"Yes, Perssa and the other heads of the families will be the first to know. They will know best how to deliver the news to the rest of their families," Dalleo replied.

"I will go to our father," Drake said. "He will likely want to meet you at Blakely's to help you."

"Then I will go to tell Skoar and Horrico," Dilen added.

The four embraced one last time, gathering strength from their fellowship, and they went their separate ways.

Dalleo walked heavily and slowly, eyes blankly staring forward toward Blakely's front grounds. How could he possibly prepare himself for such a sight as he was about to encounter? The next few moments were the loneliest Dalleo had ever felt in his entire life. As he walked on across the wood, the questions in his mind continued piling up without answers. And that, combined with recent events, made him sure that something, somewhere, was simply not right. These strange men, the cold winter, the new child, and now the death of the great Blakely...

But just as he was arriving at Blakely's front grounds, he saw a sight that was more heartbreaking than even that of seeing the lifeless Blakely. Young Jeran was frozen still in Blakely's front grounds, staring at Blakely on his stump.

'Oh, this vile, cursed day!' Dalleo thought, quite possibly aloud, and he quickened his approach.

Entering the front grounds he paused right behind Jeran and took sight of the old man himself. Shockingly, somewhere deep inside his heart, there was a sliver of joy. Although pale and empty, Blakely's face still had the look of resolve on it. Perhaps it was this look that reminded Dalleo how often Blakely would remind him, and any of the group, that death was not to be feared because it was not the end. This small hope gave Dalleo enough strength to reach out his hand and take hold of Jeran's shoulder. Jeran whipped around, and as he looked up into Dalleo's face and saw that he, too, had been crying, buried his face in Dalleo's side.

Chapter Five

Unwelcome Visitors

As the hours went on and more people came to know of the great tragedy, chaos ruled in the wood. The normal duties and chores were left undone, and sorrow and despair set in like a thick fog. There was not a dry eye amongst the people, and the only conversations taking place were recollections of fond and bittersweet memories. Small groups of people dressed in multiple animal skins had congregated in the front grounds neighboring Blakely's. They chose to stay away from Blakely's front grounds because they knew preparations were being made to take care of Blakely's body. Dalleo, his father–Essiah, and Jeran were the only people at Blakely's house, and there was little conversation between them. Dalleo had tried to console Jeran and suggested he go with his family, but Jeran stubbornly proclaimed that he was not leaving. So it became a useless battle.

While Jeran sat on a nearby stump, Essiah and Dalleo tried to decide what to do with Blakely's body. Even though Dalleo was slightly taller than his father, the resemblance would be obvious to anyone. Both men had remarkably solid physiques and both had dark hair; Essiah's was much shorter than Dalleo's. The main difference between the two was Essiah's weathered face, which showed the effects of many grueling hunting days spent in the scorching sun and the frigid snow.

The common practice in the wood after a death was to burn the body and return the ashes to the earth. Yet without the possibility of fire, Dalleo and Essiah were challenged to find an alternative. Dalleo had suggested burying the body, but Essiah strongly opposed this idea out of fear that animals would find it.

Essiah remembered a potion Horrico once mentioned that when mixed correctly could burn through most materials. With the proper combination of plants, they could still burn the body in a short period of time.

"He told me of a combination of an ivy with several other buds, some liquids and... well I don't know how it works, but it works," Essiah said.

"And how long does this process take? We do not want to be dealing with this issue all winter."

"It shouldn't take but a few days. But it has been decided; you must bring Horrico the news so we can begin as soon as possible."

"Yes, father," Dalleo said, and he turned to Jeran who was still sitting completely still on his stump. "Jeran, come with me; we have work to do. This is work Blakely would have wanted you to do."

Jeran slowly rose to his feet, never taking his eyes off of Blakely, and walked over to Dalleo. Dalleo wrapped his arm around the boy and they began walking toward the other homes of the wood.

John C. Mehl

"I know your tears," Dalleo said. "I shed the same ones."

"Why, Dalleo?" Jeran said, trying to control himself in front of the masculine presence of Dalleo. "Why did he have to die?"

"I have been asking that question myself, but I have not found the answer."

"He looked like he wasn't in pain," Jeran said, looking hopefully at Dalleo for affirmation.

"I don't think he was. It was the cold, which would make him go to sleep and not wake up."

"I can't imagine him going to sleep with his eyes open. And he hadn't his cane, for I saw it on the ground at his entryway."

This last comment froze Dalleo in his tracks. At first the conversation was simply bent on consoling the young boy, but now his own mind became greatly distressed by this boy's insight. The open eyes were one thing, but the cane could not be an ordinary coincidence. No one had ever known Blakely to be

82

without his cane for any period of time, especially when he sat on his front grounds. He was sure of it now; something had gone terribly wrong.

Some of the women had gathered in the front grounds of Hurell's home, Sharai and her mother, Perssa, included. Perssa wrapped an extra skin around Sharai and encouraged her to go rest inside to take care of herself and the child; to which Sharai obeyed and entered Hurell's home. Perssa was one of the older women of the wood, yet she did not show the effects of the years. Her face and eyes were still as bright as those of most of the younger women, and she moved around with such grace. Her golden hair and kind smile complimented her soft and gentle manner. It was no wonder there was not a member of the group who took issue with her appointment as the first woman head of any family after the death of her husband.

It was Perssa who first saw the sight that gave the other women fright. Two men, unknown to any of the women, came walking out of the trees toward them. They wore strange clothing and had large feathers sticking out of their hats. Most of the women jumped to their feet and scampered into Hurell's home, but Hurell and Perssa stepped forward to confront these men.

"Señoras, pleased to meet your acquaintance," the first man said, bending over, removing his hat, and presenting himself before the women. "I am Señor Mediche, and this is Señor Oroso. We have met several of your people just yesterday and have come to speak with them."

"Yes, we have been told of your encounter," Perssa said.

"Ah, very good then. May we please speak with the men we spoke to yesterday?" Mediche said, quickly rising from his bow and placing his hat neatly on his head.

"I'm afraid that would not be entirely possible," Perssa replied quickly. "For a great sadness has struck our wood this morning. The eldest of our group, whom you met yesterday, Blakely, was found dead this morning."

"Señora!" Mediche said, quickly removing his hat and placing it over his heart while Oroso imitated his every move. "I am terribly sorry. What a cursed day this is!"

"How was it you men found our wood?" Hurell chimed in.

"Well, it is a complicated and lengthy story," Oroso replied with lightning speed that took both Perssa and Hurell aback. "But in short, our camp was attacked by large cats, and we tracked the footprints of your men back to this wood, with some difficulty I might add."

"Well then, why don't you men follow, and we will all go to gather some of the men you spoke with yesterday," Hurell said, summoning some of the women who were listening intently from inside her home.

"Rather," Perssa said sternly, "you men must stay here, and I will gather the men for you."

As they spoke, Sharai came out of the house, well aware something was happening by the way the other women had darted into the house. At first sight of the men, she gasped, and their eyes met hers.

"Ahhh, we have met before, young lady," Mediche said, walking over to Sharai.

"Yes, sir, but what are you doing here?" she asked, shooting a look of fear to her mother.

"We were just telling these women that our camp was attacked and we tracked you back here. But before we go on, we offer our deepest condolences to you for the loss of your old friend."

"Thank you, sir," she replied in a softer voice.

"Hurell, go and get Dalleo and his brothers, and bring them back here." Perssa said.

"Mother, I am able to go and get my own husband," Sharai said.

"Young lady," Perssa said in a motherly voice. "You will go keep warm in the house; you need not trample through the heavy snow across the forest. Hurell will go and gather them." Perssa said this looking directly into Sharai's eyes and giving her a slight look that suggested there was hidden meaning behind her words.

Following Perssa's command, Hurell took off to find the brothers, and the Spaniards were invited to sit down and rest their feet.

"You men must have had quite a long journey today," Perssa said in an overtly sympathetic tone. She handed the men a small pouch of water for them to drink, and the men obliged.

"Would a bowl of warm soup please you?" she asked in a very sweet voice.

"Your kindness is overwhelming, señora. Warm soup would be splendid!" Mediche said.

Perssa rose and asked Sharai to assist her, leaving a few of the other women to keep the men

87

company. The mother and daughter went into the home and began preparing the soup.

"What are your thoughts on these men, Sharai," Perssa asked in a whisper.

"They are strange. I cannot tell if their kindness is to be trusted or not."

"Well I do not believe their intentions are honest. I doubt they could track your trail all the way from the meadow."

"Well it wouldn't be too difficult, mother. The light snow cover would make for easy tracking."

"So you believe them then?"

"I don't know what to believe. All the same, I don't really understand what harm could possibly come from believing them. What could they, two men, do to us?"

"I fear, my child, that is exactly the question they would have placed in your mind," Perssa said as she grabbed the two bowls of soup and went back outside.

Sharai plopped down on the cloth bed, which was not far from the cooking nook of the house. Each dwelling was built this same way with the beds, made up of a wood frame and cloth coverings, directly across from the cooking nook. Pouches and sacks of fruits, liquids, herbs, and such things all crowded this cooking area, leaving just enough space for the necessary meat cutting and carving utensils. In another small segment of the house, one could find a washroom–complete with a large container of water stored overhead with a spout descending within arms reach that could be opened and closed with a wooden latch as needed for washing. The excess water flowed to a hole in the ground, which was covered when not in use.

The ongoing confusion in Sharai's mind made her head ache considerably. She closed her eyes to try and ease the pain a little. A tear came to her eye as she thought that if Blakely were here, he might straighten things out. But there would be no more of that relief;

the people of the wood had lost their leader and were now left to struggle for direction and understanding.

Her thoughts caused her to drift off into a sleep, and as a result, she was a little confused when she woke and saw Dalleo kneeling by her side.

"I'm sorry, was I sleeping long?" Sharai asked, sitting up slowly.

"For some time now," Dalleo said, putting his hand on her shoulder. "I have seen the men. I don't like it, and I think something is not right."

"Not right? Well of course it's not right."

"I mean with Blakely. The timing of his death and the arrival of these men is just wrong."

"Dalleo, you don't think these men had anything to do with..." Sharai began.

"I do not believe that all of this is an odd coincidence. They are involved in this somehow."

"My dear, I think we all have had an incredibly difficult day," she said, putting her soft hand on his leg.

"You said yourself you did not trust these men, that they were dishonest," Dalleo said, rising up.

"Yes, well I may not fully understand them, but I do not believe that they came into our wood and killed Blakely," Sharai said with added emotion.

Dalleo turned to leave when Sharai stopped him.

"Where are you going?" she asked.

"The men are to stay here," he said in a frustrated tone. "My father has instructed me to begin building their quarters."

Dalleo turned and left despite several calls from Sharai.

Chapter Six

True Identities

Several days later, as the last bits of the dim sun were beginning to fade, Dalleo left the wood and made his way out to the Jessap Waters. As he sat down on a rock, Dalleo scooped up a handful of snow, bunched it up tightly, and threw it out across the water. His anger and frustration was very evident in his eyes and by his heavy and quick breathing. His thoughts ranged from the mysterious circumstances surrounding Blakely's death to his recent frustration with Sharai. Unable to find any peace in his mind, he tried to focus on something else to keep his anger from getting the best of him. He had retrieved Blakely's cane from his home before heading out to the waters and was now holding it in his hand and gazing at it just as Blakely would.

Just when Dalleo was beginning to calm his mind and his emotions, Jeran approached him and sat down beside him. The young boy, while less energetic than usual, still was much better than he had been over the last few days. He sat looking out at the rushing waters and was perfectly content with the natural noises around him substituting for any conversation between himself and Dalleo. The boy's innocence gave Dalleo no choice but to grin a little and turn his mood around. They both sat there for some time, watching the water, listening to the roar, and remembering their best moments with their best friend.

After long last, and as the harsh cold increased its sting, Dalleo turned to Jeran and said, "Thank you, friend. Your presence here truly helped me today."

"I just didn't know what to say," Jeran replied, eager to talk to Dalleo.

"Well, I think you are one of the wisest young men in all the wood."

Jeran gave a great big smile and said, "Blakely once said something like that."

Dalleo smiled back and rose to his feet, stretching after his timely period of relaxation.

"Do you think that I could…" Jeran said, pausing.

"Could what?"

"Stop by Blakely's home one more time? I mean would it be… Is he…"

"Oh, I see. Yes, Jeran, Blakely is gone. My father and Horrico took care of his… They finished the preparations. Let us go before the light is completely gone."

With that, the large man and the small boy both rose and walked back to Blakely's grounds.

When they arrived, there was barely enough light to see when inside the home. Yet Jeran still wanted to go inside and look around, and Dalleo obliged. Unlike every other home in the wood, Blakely's home had four different divisions instead of the three. In addition to the food preparation area, the sleeping quarters, and the washroom, Blakely's home had a room in which he kept all of his articles, keepsakes, and chronicles from his past. This portion would be the treasure hall for anyone as interested in Blakely's past as Jeran was.

Upon passing through the entryway, the entire right side of Blakely's home was made up of a fascinating collection of valuable relics. The very first thing people noticed as they entered the home was the great banner hanging on the far wall, made of some smooth fabric. The depiction on it was something of creative design, incorporating rushing water crashing on a large stone. It was made up of bright and earthly colors; deep greens and fluid blues, hot reds and sharp yellows. Even at dusk, this banner would shine its radiant colors throughout the room.

John C. Mehl

On either side of the banner hung two heavy swords, both alike in size and model. Above the banner hung a great shield, which had at one point bore a design on the front. Now the surface was scarred by deep cuts and scratches remaining as memories of its many battles. Several large clay containers filled with numerous rolled up parchments lined the far wall. These parchments were the wonder of the entire room, for they held the stories, the journals, and the memories from which Blakely would derive his stories, tunes, and wisdom.

This was not the first time Jeran had been in Blakely's home, and likewise not the first time he had seen Blakely's treasured possessions; he knew exactly where to go at this moment. He wanted to see these parchments that Blakely would so often refer to in his stories.

Once Dalleo understood what Jeran was after, he laughed and said, "Good choice."

Jeran picked a roll out of the clay container, sat down, and unrolled the piece of parchment, but that was as far as he got. For upon unrolling the journal, a smaller piece of parchment, which was tucked up inside the roll, floated to the ground.

"What is that?" Dalleo asked.

"I don't know," Jeran answered as he carefully picked up the parchment. "I have not seen it before."

The appearance of the parchment was alike to the journal material, only much older, and the writing was completely different. The letters were straight without any curve and were written in reflective silver ink. In fact, they were written in the same exact manner as the strange writing on Blakely's cane, a style Blakely had once said was of a land far away. Jeran slowly picked up the parchment and carefully unfurled it. He was careful not to tear the fragile antique.

The words did not make any sense at first, but then Jeran recognized a small box at the bottom of the parchment. He saw some of the strange letters alongside some of the common letters of the wood. But he could not make any sense of it, so he handed it to Dalleo.

After several minutes of inspecting it, Dalleo proclaimed, "A code! It is written in code! Each letter from this style has a common letter next to it. We can figure out what this says if we replace each word with the proper common letter."

"Why would it have to be written in code?"

"It must have been something Blakely picked up along his travels and adventures, something secret."

"Blakely kept this secret from us?" Jeran asked with disappointment.

"I will work at this tomorrow; the light is too far gone tonight. Come, Jeran, let us get you back to your parents."

Dalleo said this while carefully rolling up the parchment and leaving Blakely's house. He was completely oblivious to the disappointment Jeran was feeling.

When the two returned back to the middle of the wood, they noticed a number of people gathered around the site of Mediche and Oroso's nearly finished dwelling. Most were sitting down and some were standing, but all were listening intently. Mediche was standing up front as if he was telling some great story, and Oroso was back behind him leaning against a tree and nodding in approval. The people in the crowd were bundled up in their skins and cloths, and some were holding their small children tight. Mediche was speaking loudly and walking back and forth, wildly waving his arms around and pointing at the trees, the sky, and the ground.

While Dalleo was still too far from the scene to hear what Mediche was raving about, he approached his brothers, who were discussing something nearby.

"Hey, Drake, Dilen, what's going on?"

"These two have been at it for some time now, talking about their home and their 'civilized' ways," Drake said in an irritated tone.

"The problem is that everyone is absolutely taken in by it. They are blind to not see through the lies," Dilen added.

"What are they saying?" Dalleo asked.

"They are praising their great land of Spain and talking about the marvelous buildings and governors in that land. Without a doubt they want to take over the wood and make it their own." Drake said.

Dalleo took a couple of paces forward toward the crowd and stared at Mediche with his dark piercing eyes. Then he quickly turned and said, "Come with me."

With that, the three brothers left the group with the little boy tagging along and went back into the trees. Dalleo stopped and could only be seen by the faint light of the moon. The harsh wind blew strong and provided good cover for the words that Dalleo wished to remain secret. The four stood around in a sort of a circle; Jeran's heart was pounding with the excitement of being associated in a private discussion with these three brothers.

"I have been thinking about these men, and there is something not right about them," Dalleo whispered just loud enough to be heard over the wind.

"More than just 'something,'" Dilen remarked.

"I do not believe that they were able to simply track us here after half a day's worth of snow. I... I think they had something to do with Blakely's death."

Dalleo expected that this comment might bring forth some gasps and sharp replies, but instead there was silence for a moment.

And then Dilen said, "We agree, Dal. We were commenting earlier that there is just too much happening all at once."

"Why would they kill Blakely, though?" Drake questioned. "What had he done to them?"

"Well, I can't say about that. But I do know he did not trust them. And he had his secrets, his adventures. Maybe there is something they were after that even we do not know about."

Up until this moment Jeran had remained quiet and simply listened to the men's words, but this last comment lit a fire in him, and he exploded.

"Blakely's secrets! We thought we knew him, and it turns out that he is someone else entirely!"

"Jeran, what is the problem?" Dalleo asked, taken aback by the boy's outburst.

"He is not who he told us he was! He is someone else, someone with secrets!" Jeran lamented in a broken voice with tears welling up in his eyes.

"But it does not change who he was to us," Dilen said as he put his hand on Jeran's shoulder. "He is still Blakely."

Jeran kept quiet after this last response, but he was not ready to put this thought behind him.

"At any rate," Dalleo said, returning to his point, "I think we need to find out how involved these men truly have been in the recent happenings in the wood and what they intend to do here."

"How are we to do that?" Drake asked.

"Ask them. Their response will reveal the truth."

The meeting with the Spaniards had died down as the howling wind picked up, and people began to head back to their homes to find shelter. Mediche and Oroso were walking back to their new dwelling when they were approached in the darkness by three large figures.

"I see we have finished raising your home," said one of the figures. "May we bother you two men for a quick word?"

"Señor?" Mediche asked, squinting his eyes to see whom these men were.

"It is I, Dalleo, along with my brothers, Dilen and Drake."

"Ahhh, señor, you must forgive me; I was unsure to whom I was speaking."

"We have been wondering something about you men, and we wanted to ask you as you have been so willing to share this evening."

"Sí, whatever you would like to know."

"Have you two men anything to do with the death of our friend, Blakely?" Dalleo asked, his voice very firm and sharp.

A slight cough and a shifting of feet revealed Mediche's reaction to this response. His breathing was quick and loud as he struggled to find the words to answer the blunt question.

"Se… Señor… Wh… What?!"

"We want to know if you killed Blakely," said Dilen, who was so close to Oroso that the frightened man gave a little scream when Dilen surprised him with his presence.

"You… You think… Why I…" Oroso said with great effort.

"Are you unable to give us the truth?" Dilen said.

"Señores, you must understand," Mediche said, finally calm enough to speak clearly. "We have just come to your camp for assistance. We mean no harm."

"Well then, we have no problems," Dalleo said quietly, yet sternly as he leaned very close to Mediche's face. "Sorry to trouble you men. We are very tightly wound after the recent events."

"Yes, yes. Good evening then," Mediche said in a tone filled with uncertainty.

Mediche and Oroso entered their new home with whispers while the three men walked away in silence.

When they reached Dalleo's front grounds, they stopped. Dilen said, "Well, Dal, I did not think it would be so simple, but you were right."

"Yes, well these men are completely incapable of telling the truth. So the only question now is what do we do?" Dalleo said.

"What do we do?!" exclaimed Drake. "They killed Blakely! They deserve death! Why are we even talking about this while they lie in our own wood?"

"I understand how you feel, Drake, and I too think we need to rid ourselves of this evil tonight. Let us go and tell father and the other family heads. From there we will act."

The brothers split up, agreeing to return in a short time with several other men. Before he went to assemble his men, Dalleo entered his own home to gather, among other things, his knife and rope.

As he walked in, Sharai jumped to her feet and drew near to him.

"Dalleo, where have you been all this time? I sent people looking for you in this cold weather."

"I am sorry, my dear, but I have been busy today, and my responsibilities are not yet complete."

Dalleo quickly grabbed his needed belongings, gave Sharai a quick kiss on the cheek, and began to walk out.

"Dalleo!" Sharai exclaimed. "Why are you treating me so? What have I done to you to deserve this?"

"I am truly sorry. But I have had a lot on my mind, and you and I have not seen eye-to-eye on things lately."

"No, and I still hold that we were wrong about these men. I think they have much to offer us and that we can genuinely benefit from them."

"Sharai!" Dalleo said, dropping his things and grabbing her shoulders. "Listen to me! I... I think they killed Blakely! It was them!"

"What?! How do you know that?"

"Their lies to Drake, Dilen, and myself gave them away."

"Oh, Dalleo, you and your brothers have really gone too far this time."

"I do not have time for this. We are assembling our men and will go confront the Spaniards this evening."

"You would bring more madness and disaster to this wood because of your distrust?"

"I will protect the wood from any evil and will not allow it to remain one more night unchecked!"

With that, Dalleo stormed outside to wait for his group to join him.

Essiah was the first to show up to the meeting point. As they stood in the cold wind waiting for the others to arrive, Dalleo's conversation with his father went much more smoothly than his attempt with Sharai.

Seeing the disturbance on his son's face, Essiah said, "You sure have a lot on your mind lately, my son."

"I apologize, father. I am completely focused on our task," Dalleo replied.

Essiah began to reply, but was interrupted by a faint cry coming from inside Dalleo's home. Essiah motioned for Dalleo to go inside, but Dalleo simply shook his head and insisted that everything with the baby, Blakely, and the visitors was getting to her.

Essiah's eyes left the wood and turned to his son. "That winter before your mother died, we had many distractions as well. I will always regret that I overlooked her pain. Dalleo, you must not neglect her, especially now."

"How did you respond when mom questioned your judgment, your character?" Dalleo asked, turning toward his father.

"I wouldn't know. She never questioned my brilliance," Essiah replied in an overtly sarcastic manner.

His father's humor eased the trouble on Dalleo's mind, and both men stood on the front grounds, searching the darkness for their companions to arrive.

They continued to wait for a short time until Drake appeared in the moonlight coming near.

"Where are the others?" Dalleo called out to him.

"Dal, no one would understand. They all felt we were wrong about the Spaniards."

"Mine too," Dilen said, approaching from the opposite way. "Well, except for Ashtar and Andros here."

"Well, we have no great need for more numbers than these. Although, I would have expected a little more support from our own people," Dalleo said.

"The people of this wood have had a harsh few days. Let their confusion pass, and we will make it right for them," Essiah said, leading the group toward the home of the Spaniards.

When the men advanced on the home of Mediche and Oroso, they noticed Oroso standing outside, staring off at the forest. As they came closer, Oroso quickly approached them. His nervous breathing, as usual, revealed that there was much more going on than he would admit to.

"Señores… A problem?"

"Yes, a problem," Essiah said, taking charge of the confrontation. "You and your partner are going to have to answer to some questions, and answer truthfully, or there will be repercussions."

"But, señor, Mediche is not here. He went out to walk one of the young boys home. He had wandered…"

"Enough!" Essiah shouted loudly enough for nearby homes to hear. "We will not stand these lies one more instant! Now you will…"

"Ashtar! Andros!" exclaimed a woman, coming quickly from behind. "Have either of you seen my little Liro? He was there at the house one minute and the next he was gone!"

"Pardon, señora, but was he covered up in a small skin with a cloth cap on his head?" Oroso said, ignoring the accusations from the men and drawing near to the frantic woman.

"Yes, yes! Have you seen him?"

"Ah, yes. No worries, he was with Señor Mediche not a few moments ago, and they left to return him back to his home. I am sure they are there at this very moment."

"Oh thank you!" the woman cried, throwing her arms around the shoulders of Oroso and giving the two brothers a cold stare.

Oroso stood there consoling the woman and asked her if she would like him to accompany her home. After she told him that she would be fine and thanked him again, he finally turned back to the still angry, but perplexed men at his home.

"I cannot speak for Señor Mediche of course," he said once back amongst the men–this time with more confidence than ever before. "But I would like these accusations to stop. We have never done any harm to you men or your people, and yet your distrust for us is colder than this wind."

None of the men knew quite what to say, for the fire of their anger seemed to have disappeared in this cold night without their knowing it. While the men stood in the wind, staring blankly at each other, Oroso took one last look at the forest and entered his home. Andros and Ashtar silently broke away from the group, leaving just the father and sons to figure out how things went so awry.

"Well if these men aren't the slipperiest of serpents…" Dilen finally said.

"Their timing, their excuses, they are all far too convenient. They are too well rehearsed," Essiah added.

"We cannot continue to allow them to encamp here in our very wood!" Dalleo exclaimed, sensing the absence of their original purpose.

"We would appear the monsters to everyone in the wood should we continue," Essiah said with a heavy breath.

The father and the two brothers turned back around to head home and get out of the cold, but Dalleo stood still, glaring at the home of the enemy.

"This is not over," he said, almost growling, "not in the least."

Chapter Seven

The Messenger

The dejected men returned to their homes that night without anything to show for their efforts, yet that was not the end of business in the wood. For that night, not far from the homes, covered by thick groups of trees, two very peculiar characters stood speaking in whispers. Both wore large hats with feathers sticking out of the side. One was wrapped up in an animal skin and the other wore a long, leather cape. The man in the cape carried a large shaft in his hand and had a long, curved sword hanging from his belt. It was obvious by his appearance and speech that the man in the cape was the superior. He questioned the familiar man in animal skins and followed those questions with orders.

John C. Mehl

"They have accused you! They know what you have done, Mediche!" the caped figure said in a louder voice than his previous whispers.

This man, although a commander and superior to Mediche, did not carry himself as such. For one thing, he was terribly overweight and his clothes fit quite snugly around his body. As a result, he was forced to present himself in a less sophisticated way than his arrogance may have suggested. Like Mediche, he also had a mustache, but it was ungroomed and started to hide his lips. Without extra clothing to withstand the cold, the man's attitude and tone grew increasingly impatient and crude as late night approached.

"There are very few who suspect us, Don Villa, and those who do can be dealt with."

"I hope you are not suggesting killing them as well, Mediche. There would be no returning from that."

"No, no. We let their anger get the better of them. After our meetings with the larger group today,

116

winning over their trust and admiration, our accusers will be the outcasts; even their own families will reject them."

"You seem to understand these people pretty well for only knowing them a short period, Mediche."

"They are a simple people, and their wise man is gone now. They will be desperate for leadership and guidance."

"Well, then you must provide leaders for them. Not yourself or Oroso, for that would be too obvious. Rather support a member of the people that you can control, someone you have leverage on."

"I know just the man," Mediche said with a cruel twist in his voice. "And when will you be ready? When will our men be in place?"

"Don't question me, dog, as my equal or superior! I give you the information I choose to give you!"

"Don Villa, apologies," Mediche said, much like a scolded child.

"It will be known to you when the time is near. Do not fear. Now go and do as you are told. But remember, Mediche, you have but one chance to succeed here."

"And succeed I will, señor," Mediche said as he bowed low and turned back to the wood.

The next morning brought with it the most sunlight the wood had seen in some time. The people of the wood were out and about, taking advantage of this rare gift. Over at the edge of the wood, Jeran was just arriving at Blakely's front grounds. Still shocked and puzzled from the revelations of the previous day, he was searching for answers and hoped a trip to Blakely's house would provide some clarity.

Jeran entered Blakely's home and paused at the entryway as he looked over the old man's home. All the things that he recognized in this place now seemed different under the perspective of all that had been revealed to him. Jeran went directly toward the clay containers that held the rolls of parchment and snatched up a few. He laid them out on the floor and began reading the first. His eyes frantically searched the parchment for answers. This particular parchment was written in the common language, which Jeran could only partially understand, as he had only spent a short time with Blakely trying to learn the written language.

Jeran could only make out bits and pieces, so it did not make much sense to him. However, there was one short collection of words at the bottom of the roll that he found strikingly familiar. The collection of words was actually a list of names:

       Essiah   *Ashtar*

       Dalleo   *Andros*

       Sharai

       Perssa

Why would Blakely have a list of these people? What did they have in common? What was he planning on doing with them? All of these questions caused Jeran to feel a sort of betrayal by a 'fake Blakely.' In his mind, Jeran knew one Blakely, but each clue gave light to a completely different Blakely. Jeran started to believe that everything he ever felt, experienced, or heard from Blakely was tainted. At this moment Jeran slammed his fist on the floor, flung the rolls aside, and flew out the entryway.

He ran away from the wood toward the Jessap Waters, struggling to make his way through the high snow. When he arrived at the waters, he was completely out of breath and fell to the snow. With his mind and heart as cluttered as they were, Jeran probably did not realize what he was doing, but he yelled out loud, "Blakely! I thought I knew who you were! Why did you lie to me?"

The slight echo, faintly heard over the roar of the water as it rebounded off the high rocks, caused

Jeran to realize he had just yelled out loud. Despite his newfound distrust of Blakely and his stories, Jeran was reminded of numerous occasions in Blakely's stories when the characters could hear and talk to people that were not in the wood. Out of sheer desperation and a longing for some kind of understanding, Jeran called out to Blakely again, holding onto a small hope that the stories were at least true.

"Blakely! Why did you lie? Who were you?"

Jeran waited expectantly, but no voice would come.

"Blakely, will you not answer me now? Or were your stories and tales all lies as well?"

Again, no voice replied to Jeran's demand. Disappointment and despair began to sink in. In his rage, Jeran picked up a nearby rock and threw it as hard as he could across the water. Exhausted and overtaken with feelings of distrust and frustration, his body dropped down to the snow. Even to this moment, he had not actually had any truly malicious thoughts toward Blakely. However, as he lie there, a horribly wicked thought began to enter his mind; he was beginning to wish he had never known Blakely in the first place.

As his mind and heart dwelt on such thoughts, the roar of the water that had been so consistent seemed to become softer and softer until it was almost muted. The sharp winds began to slow until the tree branches and leaves became almost motionless. Out of the silence came a firm, but quiet, voice.

"Jeran," the voice said, "arise and speak."

Jeran raised his head and looked around for the source of the voice, but found no one there.

"Jeran, arise and speak," the voice repeated once again.

"Blakely?" Jeran asked.

"No, I am not Blakely. I am Jessap, son of King Jariel."

"Jessap?!" Jeran said, now rising to his feet. "You are *the* Jessap?"

"I am, young Jeran. And I know you, son of Skoar. I know you well."

"I thought that you disappeared. I mean, in Blakely's story, you left after speaking with him. Although, I do not know whether anything Blakely told me was the truth."

"Jeran!" replied Jessap in a stern voice. "Blakely is an honorable hero, both of your world and of mine. Do not speak evil of such a man."

"Y*our world*? What do you mean *your world*?"

"Did Blakely not explain to you of another world?"

"Well he did, but he never said it was his world."

"Which reminds me, Jeran, you must realize that though your questions may be valid and worth asking, you may not receive all the answers when you expect them."

"Wha... What do you mean?" Jeran asked, astonished that this voice would make a judgment on his character.

"You were upset because you were not told everything by Blakely, for it was not yours to know at that time. You were upset because you did not hear the voice you expected when you called out, and yet in time you came to speak with me. Patience, young Jeran. Have patience and caution with your expectations."

"Yes, sir," Jeran said, feeling the weight of the scold.

"Still, Jeran, you must listen, for there is an important role for you to take on."

"For me?"

"You must be the voice to pass on Blakely's message. You must tell those whom have been chosen what they are to do."

"Chosen for what? What are they supposed to do?"

"To make the journey to Jerudan."

"What is Jerudan?"

"Jerudan is my home. It was Blakely's home. It is the greatest city in our realm."

"How can these people make a journey from our wood to your world?" Jeran asked, mesmerized by this conversation and the wonders it was providing.

"Blakely had his orders and instructions when my father sent him to your world with me. In those instructions, you will find what have now become your orders, young Jeran, orders that came directly from the king."

"The king has given me orders? How does the king know me?" Jeran said with excitement.

"He does not personally know you. He has been told of you, and he has heard much about you."

"Who told him of me?"

"Blakely, of course. Blakely told the king that should he ever be unable to carry out his orders, you would be the one to take his place."

This last comment drew such a mixture of emotions from Jeran that he was unable to say anything for some time.

"The orders will be clear, but you must make sure you do not speak idly about this to anyone that is not directly involved. You have been chosen, Jeran, and this is to be your service to the king."

"I will be careful," Jeran said. "But what am I to do first?"

As Jeran was waiting for a response to his last question, the roar of the waters increased, and the wind blew strong and fierce once again. Jeran waited for a response that would never come; he continued calling out for Jessap again and again. When he at last realized the miraculous conversation was over, he sat back down, gathering all of his thoughts. He first began to regret his doubt of Blakely and the negative thoughts that had crossed his mind. Seeing Blakely in a new light and hearing how his old friend spoke of him to the king, Jeran realized that Blakely was, as

Jessap said, a hero. It was out of this renewed respect and loyalty to Blakely that Jeran decided he would obey his orders from the king.

Inspired by his newfound vigor and purpose, Jeran picked himself up and darted back toward the wood.

Dalleo was clearing the snow from his front grounds when Sharai appeared in the entryway of their home. When Dalleo noticed her presence, he sighed deeply and approached her. The soft look on her beautiful face demonstrated the grace she hoped to find in Dalleo.

"I want to be able to speak with you again," she said gently.

"As do I," Dalleo replied.

"I understand your frustration and your feelings concerning all that is occurring. I do not mean to fault you for your beliefs, but I do not want the entire wood to undergo more strife than it already has."

"Sharai, you must listen to me. You have trusted me with all things, including the birth of our child, and you must trust me with this. These men have killed Blakely!"

"Oh, Dalleo, you make my situation so hopeless when you make me choose between siding with you and keeping you from tearing the wood apart."

Dalleo put his head down and took a deep breath, for it was very apparent that neither was willing to compromise their beliefs. The only thing that kept the conversation from turning into an argument was Jeran dashing through their front grounds toward Dalleo. His appearance and the look on his face were such a change from the last time Dalleo had seen him that Dalleo assumed something important would follow.

Struggling to catch his breath, the young boy said, "Dalleo, I must speak with you!"

"What is it, Jeran, that put a smile on your solemn face of late?"

"It is about what we were discussing yesterday," Jeran said, clearly withholding much out of uncertainty of whom he could speak with about such things.

Sharai took the hint and entered the house in a huff. Dalleo watched her go and battled within himself with the decision of finishing their ongoing conversation or listening to the boy. However, Jeran's next comment made the decision for him.

"I have spoken with Jessap this day."

"You have wha…" Dalleo said, taken aback by the wonder of the boy's remark.

"Down at the Jessap Waters. I spoke to him!"

"How could you… You saw him?"

"No, but it was like the old stories. He spoke to me."

"What did he have to say?"

"He told me all sorts of things. But first, you must figure out what the parchment we found yesterday really says."

"Well, I looked at it this morning and it does not make much sense to me."

"What could you make out?" Jeran asked, pushing harder for Dalleo to get involved.

"It spoke of some kind of instructions involving ashes and water. Does that make any sense to you?" Dalleo asked, a little amused that he was seeking answers from the younger Jeran.

"Well… Not really. But it will. Come with me!"

Jeran darted out of the front grounds and back into the center of the wood. Dalleo took one look back to his home and followed the boy at a similar pace.

When they arrived at Blakely's front grounds, Jeran was giddy with excitement, but Dalleo had stopped and was staring back out at the home of Mediche and Oroso. The two men were outside straightening up their front grounds with the help of several members of the wood. After constant summons by Jeran, Dalleo finally turned and entered the home, yet the feelings of fury toward the Spaniards continued to linger.

Jeran laid all of the parchments out on the floor in a very scattered manner and began explaining the substance of his discussion with Jessap.

"…And then he told me that it was to be my duty to the king. And that was it," Jeran said after his lengthy explanation.

"Blakely is of another world, this Jerudan?" Dalleo asked, trying to take all of this in.

"Yes, and I still find it so hard to believe," Jeran said, very excited to be having this conversation with a 'regular' human.

"Well, it may make more sense than not," Dalleo said in such a tone that suggested his mind was working feverishly to uncover the entirety of this mystery.

"How's that?"

"Well, Blakely has always been around since our people arrived in the wood. Who knows where he was before that."

"I guess I never thought of it like that," Jeran said.

"And it also explains the stories of Jessap returning home. When we heard those stories, we simply assumed that his home was in this world. Why shouldn't his home be in this other world, this Jerudan? And his cane… his cane!!!"

"What of his cane?"

"His cane… with the writing… and the writing!!!"

At this point, Dalleo's mind was moving so quickly that the boy was completely left behind. So when Dalleo finally slowed down, he had to catch Jeran up.

Once the boy was caught up, he tried to summarize their last few minutes.

"So Blakely received his cane from an old friend at home, the king. And the cane had his orders for when to return written on it?" Jeran asked.

"And that writing," continued Dalleo, "is the same writing that appears on the parchment we found with the instructions of ash and water. Therefore, the instructions must be somehow related to a journey to Jerudan."

Up until this point, Jeran had only told Dalleo that there *were* names on a list, but not *whose* names they were. In all the excitement of the rest of the mystery, he had completely forgotten the significance of those names. He now realized that the people on the list were to make the journey. The next thing that hit his mind was a harsh reality; his name was not on the list. Jeran was supposed to follow the orders of the king; he was supposed to be Blakely's voice to the chosen people, but he was not on the list of those chosen to make the journey? This troubled him greatly, and Dalleo noticed the sudden change in attitude.

"You know, Jeran, if you continue to switch moods back and forth like this, I will never be able to catch up."

"The names... The names of the people that are on Blakely's list are to make the journey to Jerudan."

"Ahh, yes. That is right! Well then, who are they?

"Well... you and Sharai... your father and Perssa... and others I can't remember."

"We are to make the journey?!" Dalleo marveled, completely taken aback with a mixture of extreme shock and joy.

"Not we... you," Jeran said in a mournful tone.

"Your name is not on the list? How can that be?"

"I am just to obey orders and be left here."

"Well left here with your family, with the wood, with the other families."

"Not all of the families."

"Look, Jeran," Dalleo said, lowering to one knee and putting an arm on the shoulder of the boy. "I do not know why your name is not on the list, but I do know that the king has specifically chosen you, and that counts for something."

With this encouragement from Dalleo combined with his memory of the light scolding he had received from Jessap, Jeran lightened his mood and continued to look over the rolls of parchment.

The two of them looked like children trying to solve a puzzle on the floor–which was almost exactly what they were doing. They had just begun to match some of the letters of the common language with symbols of the language of Jerudan when they heard a call from outside Blakely's home.

"Señores!" came the call of Mediche.

Both Jeran and Dalleo jumped and began to quickly hide away the parchments, as they did not want these men to discover their secret.

After some time, they both came out of the house and met the men on the front grounds. Mediche was wearing a new skin, given to him by a member of the Essiah family. Oroso wore a cloth cape that wrapped around his whole upper body and hung down to his feet. In Oroso's hands was a familiar shaft, all shiny and in good condition. Dalleo noticed the unusual garb and inquired of the occasion that called for such sophisticated attire.

"Ahh, we are off on a hunting voyage with some of your family, Dalleo. We wanted to know if you would come along."

"Busy with chores," Dalleo said shortly, continuing to stare at the shaft in the hands of Oroso.

"Pity," Oroso said. "We could use strong hands such as yours."

"What need have you of hands with that shaft as your weapon?"

"Well then, we are off," Oroso said, ignoring the pointed question.

The men walked off, followed closely by several members of the group, who were excited to be on a hunt with these men. Most in the wood had, by this time, come to welcome the Spaniards. They particularly welcomed the stories of civilization and the land of Spain. The people had always loved listening to the great tales Blakely told, and they were happy to find that they had not completely lost everything they loved when Blakely passed. There were now new storytellers among the group. The Spaniards' stories of far off lands and adventures filled a great void. In a sense, the people of the wood began to give the Spaniards the social role Blakely had filled without pausing to consider the end result.

Dalleo and Jeran were not of this mentality and despised the fact that their kinsmen were accepting the Spaniards so willingly. But presently, there were other things on their minds, and the two got back to their work on the parchments.

At long last, Dalleo jumped up and exclaimed, "Jeran, this is it!"

Jeran rushed over to Dalleo's side to see what he was all wound up about. He saw that Dalleo had converted much of two rolls of parchment into the common language. The two rolls lie side by side with Blakely's cane lying over both of them. The smaller of the two was the roll that contained the code to decipher the two languages. The other was a new parchment that Dalleo had written on himself.

Dalleo's generally calm and collected personality was now completely gone, and he became intensely energized and animated at his most recent discovery.

"It's his ashes, Jeran! His ashes!" Dalleo shouted. "They are the way to Jerudan."

"His ashes? How can... But they are... What?" Jeran asked very confused and slightly disturbed that the topic of conversation was the ashes of a dear friend.

"This parchment," he said, holding up the smaller of the two, "is full of instructions on how Blakely was to make the trip from Jerudan to this wood. It says he was to take the ashes of the king's father and spread them in the water. Then he would jump into the water himself, and he, along with the ashes, would be sent back to this world. It is actually a simple plan."

"But how could the ashes send people from one world to another?"

"That," Dalleo said, excited at being asked this question, "is why we have this other parchment. This tells us that the father of the king was actually from this world and was taken to Jerudan many years ago because of a demon army. Since his body belongs to this world, it would naturally return if given the chance. And it says here that this 'chance'–this 'chance,' young Jeran, requires the common element of the wood and Jerudan."

"Does it say what the common element is?" Jeran asked, catching onto the excitement.

"No, but it is clear from these instructions that Blakely was to spread the ashes of the father in the water!"

"The Jessap Waters!" Jeran said, jumping to his feet. "Of course! Blakely was always spending time down at the Jessap Waters."

"This is some divine mystery!" Dalleo said, bewildered by the enormity of these discoveries.

Dalleo walked over to the entryway and looked out at the frozen wood, seeing people moving to and fro on their business. He thought of the families, his family, and his friends, and how everything around him was changing. He thought of Sharai and their child, of their recent arguments and anger. He thought of Mediche and Oroso and of their evil doings. He thought of all these things and was astonished at how different this was from the peaceful wood of only a season ago.

It seemed as if the wood itself were a different place now. The people were acting as if they belonged to a different home, and the wood of old was only a distant memory. All the talk and focus in the wood was now on becoming a 'new' people, a 'better' and 'civilized' people. All the longing and yearning for Blakely's fireside stories froze along with the winter air and was replaced by the cold reality of the outside world, as presented by Mediche and Oroso.

This train of thought would likely have continued on for some time if Dalleo had not just seen Sharai approaching the front grounds. The look on her face was not a pleasant one, which was all too common in recent days.

"Dalleo, you have responsibilities at our own home that you have left unattended for too long now."

"Sharai," Dalleo said, setting aside her intended topic of conversation. "There is great and wonderful news." He walked near to her and sat her down on a nearby stump. He kneeled beside her and softly held her hands in his for the first time in a long while. The excitement and wonder in his eyes went unmatched in Sharai's confused, but still beautifully bright, eyes.

"What is it that has you so worked up today," Sharai said in a cold manner.

"It is a most incredible mystery that we have discovered in exploring the belongings left by Blakely. Yet you must keep your thoughts clear and without judgment until I am finished."

"No doubt this will be more of your wild logic, but continue," she said, crossing her arms and leaning back a little.

"We have found something, something incredible!" Dalleo said, still kneeling and holding Sharai's hands.

"We?" Sharai asked, looking around Dalleo for this 'other person' he was apparently referring to.

"Jeran and I," Dalleo said, noting her aggravated response. "We have found something involving Blakely that you must know."

At the mere mention of the name Blakely, Sharai finally shook off her irritated demeanor and now appeared interested. Despite her bitterness with her husband, her emotions toward the old man were still very tender, and she softened as she thought of him. Her eyes exposed this change in attitude, and this gave Dalleo the courage to continue.

"We have found some news that reveals things about Blakely that we did not know. Nobody knew these things. He was not of this wood after all, but from another land entirely. A land of kings and demons and all the sort from his stories."

"Yes, well he was not from the wood. That is no great surprise."

"My dear, that is not the main issue at hand. The point is that his land, the land of Jerudan, is not of this realm. It is of another domain entirely, another world!"

Dalleo said this looking intently into Sharai's eyes in order to discern her thoughts. However, he didn't need to make such an effort, for the look in her eyes would have been obvious to a stranger. Her soft and eager demeanor instantly changed to annoyed and cold as she pulled her hands away from Dalleo and turned her face. As this reaction was not completely unexpected, Dalleo tried in vain to regain her focus.

"Sharai, I know that it may sound foolish, yet it is the truth."

"Too far, Dalleo. Much too far this time with your ridiculous logic."

"You doubt the clarity of my mind?" Dalleo asked forcefully at the attack on his integrity.

"That is just it. I do not doubt for a moment that you are honest in your beliefs. But I will not follow you in this foolish and childish mentality that you have of Blakely and Mediche and everything else lately."

"You mean to say that it is not these truths you are rejecting, but me in general?" Dalleo said partially in anger and partially in pain.

"Something in you has changed, Dalleo, and I cannot understand what it is. It seems as if every time

I speak with you there is some wild idea coming out of your mind, and nothing is real with you."

"You have lost your faith in me? That is what this is! Well how can we raise a child together if you cannot believe in me or trust that I know what is best for this family, for this entire wood?"

This rage frightened both Sharai and Jeran, who had come out of the house as the volume of the argument grew. Dalleo quickly rose up, his towering figure bulging and throbbing with the pounding of his heart. His fiery eyes glared at Sharai with an anger she had never seen before–at least she had never before seen it directed at her. His heavy breathing and clinching of his hands exposed the fact that Dalleo had lost control of his emotions and fury had taken over.

With one last enraged glare and a grunting heavy breath, Dalleo thundered out of the front grounds and into the forest, leaving Jeran and Sharai frozen in terror.

Chapter Eight

Betrayal

Sharai had left the front grounds of what used to be a home she could always come to for guidance and peace. Yet on this day, it only brought fear, confusion, and pain. She fell down to the snow in a mess of tears and emotional exhaustion. Burying her face in her hands, she wept uncontrollably for some time, remembering the terrifying look of rage in the eyes of her beloved Dalleo. She could not help but feel she had been the cause and had completely betrayed him and left him helpless. At the same time, she could not bring herself to comprehend why his mind was so lost in such foolish and irrational thoughts. He had always been as true as anyone when it came to reason and reality, yet now it appeared as if he was rejecting them both. Thus, Sharai concluded that the death of Blakely must have shaken him more than she knew.

Sobbing and lost in uncertainty, Sharai was oblivious to Mediche's approach until he was kneeling down right beside her, placing his hand on her head. Her head jolted up and a little shriek escaped her lips at the shock of the man's close presence. Mediche only smiled and gently rubbed her head. Sharai quickly rose to her feet and tried to wipe the frozen tears from her face.

"Señora, you are far too beautiful to have such mournful tears. And being with child, you must allow me to accompany you home into warmth," Mediche said, rising and holding onto her hand.

"Thank you, sir," Sharai said, standing to her feet. "It's just…" she paused, uncomfortable about opening up her situation and emotions to this man.

"Go on, señora, you can confide in me."

"Dalleo…Well… He is just not making any sense to me lately."

"Ah, yes," Mediche said with a hint of spite in his voice. "I have had some unfortunate encounters with him as well. I trust he has not hurt you at all."

"Never would he deliberately hurt me, but he is so distant from me right now. His mind is on such strange things."

"Strange?" Mediche said inquisitively.

"Well…" Sharai said, unsure of how much she wanted to reveal to this man.

"Señora, if you find that you cannot confide in your man, I am ready and willing to listen to whatever you may want to say. I think you may find that I am very understanding."

"Thank you, sir," Sharai said with a deep sigh, unwilling to hold back any more of her thoughts or feelings.

The two of them walked deeper into the forest. Mediche wrapped Sharai in the skin he had been wearing and walked slowly with his arm around her, listening intently to every part of her story. He was no longer encouraging her to go home and warm up.

Meanwhile Dalleo was stomping through the snow back to his home, still enraged and deeply wounded. As he approached his home, his father came out to meet him. Once he saw the appearance of his son and the anguish on his face, he assumed that the troubles with Sharai had only worsened. Saying nothing, he walked back to the front grounds with Dalleo and sat down, allowing his son to deal with the issue in his own way.

"She has lost faith in me, father," Dalleo said after some time of blank stares and heavy breaths.

"She loves you, son; there is no doubt there," Essiah said softly as he leaned back against a tree.

"No, father! There is great doubt! She will not believe me. She will not follow me!"

"Well, where is it that you are trying to lead her?"

Realizing that his next words would contain much more than a simple response, Dalleo sat up and took a deep breath, turning directly toward his father.

"I have found things out, father. There were aspects about Blakely's life that may be a little hard to understand, or even comprehend. He... He was not from this wood, not even from this land, this world."

Expecting a hesitant or skeptical response, Dalleo searched his father's eyes and face for his reaction. To his surprise, his father had little reaction at all, save a raised gray eyebrow and a slight humming noise as he continued to lean against the tree in anticipation of more explanation.

"This does not affect you, father, the way it did Sharai."

"Yes, well I have heard and seen enough of the old stories to come to expect the abnormal and seemingly unrealistic aspects of the truth."

"So you believe... I mean you understand me, father?" Dalleo said with contentment.

"I may, when you continue your explanation, unless that is the end of it," he said with a smile that embraced the broken heart of his son.

"Young Jeran and I found and deciphered some of Blakely's old parchments," Dalleo continued eagerly. "We have discovered that Blakely came from a land called Jerudan and was the adviser to the king. That king was actually the father of Jessap, who came to this very wood with Blakely for protection from enemy forces during a great war."

Dalleo paused again, waiting for a reaction from his father. When his father remained silent, but still fully attentive, Dalleo said, "I am afraid you are thinking me mad."

"My son," Essiah whispered as he leaned forward, "I have found that stories make much more sense at the end, when everything has been laid out. I am a patient man, so please continue."

"Well, Jeran has the most pivotal part of the story, but as he is not here to tell it, I must. He actually spoke with Jessap himself! Not in body, but his voice. Jessap told him that Blakely had orders that Jeran must now complete. We discovered those orders back in Blakely's house on a parchment that I had to transcribe into the common words. They are instructions on how Blakely could travel from Jerudan to this wood. The instructions also contain a list of names, people chosen to make the trip back to Jerudan."

"Which of our people were chosen to make this trip?" Essiah asked, satisfied that he had heard enough of this account to chime in and ask questions.

"Well, you—father and myself and Sharai…" he said, pausing at the mention of her name.

"And others?" Essiah asked, trying to avoid losing Dalleo to his emotions.

"Yes, father. Yet I am not sure who they are since Jeran still has the list."

"When is this journey to be made? Do the orders clarify that?"

"That is just it, father. The orders are written upon Blakely's old cane in a sort of rhyme or verse. They are written in strange writing that now can be transcribed with a key found in another parchment."

"And the journey…" Essiah said, reminding his son of his question.

"It reads on his cane that the journey is to take place in the coldest winter when nothing can burn."

"Well this is undoubtedly that winter. How is the journey to be made?"

"I found a separate parchment that speaks of using the ashes of one who is not of this world and combining them with water, as it is apparently the common element of this land and that. If we are present or touching the ash as it is combined with the water, I suppose we will be taken to Jerudan as well."

"There is no question of that," Essiah said, correcting his son. "We know that it works true, as

153

it brought Blakely here to the wood. It appears to me that the time has come upon us to make these things happen. Jessap speaking with Jeran, the extremity of the winter, and the arrival of the outsiders; the time, my son, is now."

Greatly encouraged by the support and wisdom of his father, Dalleo rose to his feet and said, "I will go speak with Jeran and tell him that it is time to fulfill his orders."

With that, Dalleo strode out toward the center of the wood when his father stopped him to ask, "And what of Sharai?"

Dalleo turned and replied, "She did not believe me before. Why would she be willing to make such a journey with our baby on the way?"

"She has a good heart and a clear mind, son. The two will meet to bring her understanding."

"And what if she will not go, father? What if she refuses to understand?"

"Then you will deal with that if it comes. But do not make the same mistake she is making right now; trust her."

Dalleo nodded, understanding his father's advice, then turned and left to seek Jeran.

Dalleo found Jeran still on the front grounds at Blakely's home, holding the cane as Blakely had done. The sight of this made Dalleo smile as he approached the boy. Jeran looked up and watched Dalleo intently, trying to discern the mood of the man. Seeing a much more calm and controlled face, Jeran rose and met him.

"Sharai left some time ago to the forest. I have not seen her come back."

"I will go look for her in a moment. But first, I think it is time that you fulfill your orders from the king, Jeran. I spoke with my father and told him everything. He believes that with the extremity of the winter and the happenings in the wood, the time is now."

"Now, as in tonight?!" Jeran exclaimed.

"You take your list and meet with the people, and I will go to find Sharai. After you have told them, they will want to talk with my father. Have them all meet us at the fire pit at dark, making sure to share this with no one else."

"Why keep it a secret?"

"The wood is not as it used to be. Our people are unsure of who they are and are seeking guidance from the outsiders. We do not want to try and explain all of this to them at this point, less it separate us more."

"I will tell the others to keep it secret," Jeran said, now feeling anxious of his upcoming task.

"Now go and fulfill your duty," Dalleo said with a smile as Jeran scurried off the front grounds.

Dalleo turned and headed toward the forest. After only a few steps, he paused. Coming toward him from the forest was Sharai with Mediche next to her. Sharai was wearing Mediche's skin and his arm was around her shoulder keeping her warm. The look on her face when she saw Dalleo was one of sorrow and lament, and yet his face returned to the rage that she had last seen. He swiftly approached the man and, without warning, struck a blow to his face that knocked him back into the snow. Sharai yelled at Dalleo, trying to make him stop, yet his ferocity had already taken over. He picked the bleeding and moaning man up from the snow and threw him against a nearby tree, smacking his head with a great thud.

"Your first mistake was assuming that you could fool me! Your second mistake was laying a hand on her! There will not be another!" he roared as he smacked Mediche's head once more against the tree. "I will not let you corrupt this wood with your presence for one more second!"

A sharp scream came from Sharai that was unlike her previous pleads and wails; it was enough to cause Dalleo, even in his fury, to stop and look at her. Sharai fell to the ground, eyes closed and tears on her cheek. In one move, Dalleo threw Mediche to the ground and went to her. She was not moving. Despite Dalleo's constant calls, she would not open her eyes. Picking her up, he stammered into Blakely's home, leaving the bloodied and battered Mediche moaning on the ground.

Chapter Nine

'Introductions'

Inside Blakely's home, Dalleo gently placed Sharai on the ground and grabbed cloths and skins to cover her. Her face was pale. He kissed her forehead repeatedly and wiped away her tears. Dalleo pleaded with her to open her eyes as he held her head in his hands. Her eyes twitched once, twice, and then opened slightly. Sharai moaned in pain and called out Dalleo's name.

"I am here, love. I am here."

"Dalleo..." she said in a faint voice, and her eyes closed again.

"Señor Dalleo," came a call from outside the home.

Dalleo simply ignored the call and continued to try and wake Sharai.

"Dalleo," came the unexpected, distressed voice of his father.

Dalleo turned and saw through the entryway a battered Mediche crouching behind his father with a knife to Essiah's throat. Torn between taking care of his wife and killing this wicked man, Dalleo remained in his crouched position at Sharai's side.

"Come, or this man will die," Mediche said in a tone that he had not used in the wood before.

Dalleo slowly rose to his feet, softly let go of Sharai's hand, and walked out the entryway. The next few moments occurred so quickly that it was difficult for Dalleo to understand what happened. As Dalleo stepped out, he saw not only his father, but also Perssa, Ashtar, and Andros, all those whose names had appeared on Blakely's list. They were surrounded by a large group of dark men, some with knives and some with large hunting shafts. These men had similar faces to that of Mediche and Oroso, dark with carefully styled facial hair. They wore heavy black cloths draped over their shoulders, and large feathered hats covered their heads. Upon seeing this treacherous sight, Dalleo lunged out at Mediche, but he did not make it even half of his intended distance. The moment he jumped out, a deafening crack exploded and he was struck down. Shocked and in great pain, he looked down only to see blood seeping out from a wound across his thigh.

Dalleo grunted in pain as a man standing in the front grounds yelled in a thick accent, "Lucky that one only skimmed your leg!"

Seconds later the man was struck and scolded by a large, fat man, who was even more strangely dressed than the rest. He wore a hat similar to that of his companions, but his feather was much larger and more extravagant. The cloth draped over his shoulder was richly ornamented with gold chains and medallions laden with jewels. His size caused him to move slowly in more of a waddle than a walk. In contrast to the angry scowls of all the other men, a sly grin could be seen on his dark face.

Dalleo lifted his eyes to his father, who was looking back with a fierce stare. Struggling to stand, Dalleo called out, "Sharai! I am coming!" Before he could move, the fat man approached and stood over him.

"I, señor, am Don Villa of Spain. I regret that my man has taken such foolish measures to stop you. He will be severely reprimanded for his actions."

Don Villa spoke with a depth in his voice that was appropriate for such a large figure. Because of his size, he was unable to crouch next to Dalleo, so he simply spoke down to him from his standing position. His manner was very relaxed despite the chaos of the past moments, so he did not appear threatening.

"Who are you? Why have you come to this wood?" Dalleo asked, struggling through the pain.

"Let us not move too fast, señor, for we are still busy with introductions. Tell me, what is your name?"

Dalleo refused to answer, but grabbed his leg in order to position it so that he could stand. Don Villa, noticing his struggles, snapped at two of his men, who came running to help Dalleo up. As they came near, Dalleo yelled at them to back away. He half-hobbled, half-crawled to a stump and used it to prop himself up. He was about to address Don Villa when he heard a cry from inside the house.

"Dalleo!" Sharai cried, "Dalleo!"

Gathering all the strength he possessed in his monstrous body, Dalleo staggered over to the entryway. He looked in to see Sharai still laying on the floor, but struggling in great pain. He tried too quickly to make his way over to her and fell to the ground. From the floor, he crawled over close to her and wiped away the sweat that had formed on her brow.

"What is it, my love? You are in pain!" he said.

"As are you."

"Forget about me. What is wrong?"

"It is the child, Dalleo. It is coming now," Sharai gasped.

Dalleo's mind was moving so quickly that he completely ignored the situation outside and called out for his father. Don Villa nodded his approval and Mediche released his hold on Essiah, who ran into the home. Quickly seeing that the wound on his son was not so severe as to threaten his life, Essiah tended to Sharai.

"Get some water and some cloths!" he ordered Dalleo.

Dalleo struggled across the home, crashing and stumbling the whole way.

Meanwhile, in the front grounds, Perssa had talked her way free from the clutches of the Spaniards and quickly entered the home. Grasping the situation, she hurried to help Dalleo. When they returned with the water and the cloths, Essiah was kneeling next to Sharai, whispering comforting words in her ear.

"He is here, Sharai. He still loves you, you and the child."

Seeing that Dalleo had returned, she cried, "I have betrayed you! I have completely deceived you!"

"Shhh..." Dalleo said, trying to calm her down. "You are fine."

"I brought this trouble here. I betrayed everyone!"

"What are you saying, love?"

"I distrusted you and was disloyal. I confided in Mediche all that you had told me, everything Dalleo! And now I have betrayed my family, my home, my love!" She cried and immersed herself in tears and despair.

"Nothing you have done or could ever do would ever separate you from me. I am here at this moment, and our child is coming. Focus on that, Sharai; nothing else is important right now."

Moments passed by that seemed like days, and minutes passed like an eternity, and still Sharai was lying on the floor with her mother and Essiah watching over her, taking care of her. Dalleo remained by her side, reassuring her as he cleaned his own wounded leg. This continued for the rest of the day and well into the night. It seemed to those inside Blakely's home that the previous events outside had never really occurred. However, to those outside the house, the events of the day were a completely different experience.

Right after Essiah and Perssa followed the stumbling Dalleo into the house, Andros and Ashtar began to question the Spaniards and their intentions. The angry commotion drew the neighbors' attention, and they began to gather around. When Don Villa could not satisfy their anger with his belittling remarks and apologetic words, he simply removed his men, taking them out to the middle of the forest for a meal and more 'introductions.' Mediche and Oroso stayed behind and caught a great tirade from the people who felt insulted and betrayed for having befriended and welcomed them. The confrontations ended when Ashtar had to restrain Andros from taking a swing at Mediche, which was as much for Mediche's protection as it was for Andros'. Then, for the first time all day, the wood was quiet; not calm, but quiet.

The quiet only lasted a moment before it was broken by the cry of a small child from within the Blakely home. The tears of pain and suffering that had fallen down Sharai's face were now tears of joy and amazement. She was gazing at Dalleo as he held the small, crying baby boy in his large hands and whispered terms of affection to him. Perssa was also beaming at this sight, while Essiah continued to care for the exhausted Sharai.

"He already looks like you, Dalleo," Sharai said, exhaling deeply. "He has your dark hair."

"No," Dalleo said, looking into the squinting eyes of his son. "He may have my hair, but he has your eyes."

"He will follow you and grow to be a great man," Perssa added.

"We will all follow you," Sharai said, looking at Dalleo apologetically.

"And how will he be known? What is the name that his friends will cherish and enemies will fear?" Essiah asked with a smirk.

"Well, we have not really…" Sharai began.

"Blake," interrupted Dalleo. "His name will be Blake."

Sharai's quick smile and sudden squeeze of Dalleo's hand signaled her approval.

The four of them sat there for some time, marveling at this miracle within the wood. At long last, Essiah pulled Perssa aside and explained to her the discoveries of Jerudan and her involvement.

After Essiah had finished explaining as accurately as he could, the delighted Perssa stated, "If Blakely has chosen us for this, we must follow his guidance."

Essiah took another look at Dalleo's wounded leg, finished cleaning it, and covered it up with a new cloth.

"What was it that hit you?" he asked.

"The same sort of fire-rock that killed the buck."

"After all of the games and tricks they tried to play, I still would not have thought their plan was to take control of the wood," Essiah said with a grunt.

"Dalleo," Sharai said, looking up from her baby. "I am sorry I could not see through their act. I was…"

"My love, speak not another word of it. We are here now, and things are as they are."

"Yes, but now they know all about Blakely's secrets."

"They will certainly attack that truth first," Essiah added. "That will be the greatest threat to their attempts to take control."

"Then the longer we wait, the more time they will have to settle among us and continue to deceive the others," Dalleo said.

"Wait for what?" Sharai asked.

"My dear, I was unable to tell you the whole truth earlier," Dalleo said, turning to Sharai and grasping her hand. "Blakely made a list of people who are to make a journey to Jerudan, and he has chosen us among others."

"To Jerudan? But is that not outside of this world? Dalleo, we just brought our child into this world. Even a short journey would be dangerous for him, and you want to travel to an unknown world?"

"I understand and have had the same doubts myself," Dalleo said solemnly.

"But you must," Essiah said. "This wood is falling into the control of the Spaniards. Even if we stay, we will not be able to save the wood."

"Then why not move on and travel to another part of the range?" Sharai asked.

"Not this winter. We couldn't survive the cold apart from the resources and shelter we have here," Essiah replied.

"And how far is Jerudan? How would we make this journey? Is it safe?" Sharai asked frantically as Perssa wiped a wet cloth over her head to calm her.

"Regardless, my love, it is a journey we have been chosen to make. And still, I don't believe Blakely would have chosen us to embark in this way if all would not be right in the end," Dalleo said, firmly holding her hand.

"I... I don't..." Sharai stammered and then stopped. Looking into Dalleo's eyes, she remembered all the occurrences of the day and said, "Where you lead, I will follow."

Dalleo embraced her tightly and gently rubbed the head of his child, who was all bundled up in cloths.

"Father, how was it that these men were able to take you, and you, Perssa, under their control?" Dalleo asked, turning toward the two elders.

"Well you see, Jeran had just met with Ashtar, telling him to meet at the fire pit, when that man, Oroso, stopped him in his tracks and questioned him. Jeran simply said that he was delivering a message, but Oroso did not buy the story. He told Jeran that he had become aware of the foolish gatherings and meetings. He tried to grab the boy when Ashtar struck him from behind, and Jeran ran off. As Ashtar called out for help, about fifteen Spaniards came out from the forest. They had Ashtar surrounded before he could get away. I was not far off and could hear the cries for help. I grabbed Andros and we ran toward the noise, but we were overtaken and forced to the ground by knifepoint.

"That is when that large man, Don Villa, appeared out of the forest with a sinister look on his face," Essiah continued. "He told us that he was a friend and was not here to hurt anyone, but he could not tolerate our rash and violent actions. It was then that one of his men quickly approached him and whispered something in his ear. After that, he spoke to his men in some words I could not understand, and we were whisked away here. When we were in the front grounds, Mediche showed up, grabbed me, and called to you. I noticed by the sound of his voice, not to mention the beating I assumed you had given him, that he was no longer trying to appear innocent."

"They will surely answer for this treachery," Dalleo remarked firmly.

"If we leave the wood, what will become of those left behind?" Sharai asked, looking up from her child.

"Can we really just leave them with these men still in the wood?" Perssa questioned.

"That may not be our choice to make," Essiah replied. "All we can do is follow where we have been led. I will talk to the others, to Dilen and Drake and try to explain everything to them."

"Father, do you expect that these men will allow us to move freely through the wood?" Dalleo asked.

"Not likely. We will have to keep our movements hidden and disguised."

"Then you must move now, but I must stay here with Sharai."

"No, Dalleo," Sharai said, grasping his hand. "You go with your father; I will be fine."

"I will stay and take care of her," Perssa added.

"Come, son," Essiah said, rising to his feet. "We will return here shortly, and you women must be ready at that time to leave."

"We will be ready," Perssa answered as she wiped down Sharai's face and gently caressed the soft head off her grandson.

Dalleo took some time in leaving, as he gave a long kiss to Sharai and stared in adoration at his beautiful, young Blake.

Chapter Ten

'Follow One More Step'

Leaving Sharai and the baby at home was not an easy task for Dalleo, yet after some time, he and his father were outside on Blakely's front grounds looking over the surroundings. The night was as cold as any other, and a thin layer of clouds veiled the dim light of the moon. The surrounding wood was completely vacant, yet not silent. Loud and obnoxious shouts and bellows could be heard from the nearby newcomers. The sound of the voices allowed Essiah and Dalleo to determine the exact location of the group, giving them the ability to move about with more ease.

"We will go around their camp toward Ashtar and Andros."

"Should we not split up and cut our time in half?"

"No, we must stay together. You, with your leg, are not well, and we must not encounter any trouble by ourselves, lest we be without excuse or explanation."

With that, both men trekked through the snow and headed out away from the wood toward the thick tree cover.

Keeping their movement as stealth as possible, the men crept slowly and steadily between the trees, constantly keeping their eyes on the wood as they tried to avoid drawing attention. The darkness might have handicapped an average man's attempt to sneak through the forest, but Dalleo and Essiah's vast experience made them more than capable of moving quickly and effectively toward their destination.

As they approached Ashtar's home, they could see him outside speaking with his brother, Andros.

Dalleo gave a birdcall, attempting to gain their attention. At this, both men faced the trees and found Dalleo and Essiah barely exposing themselves from concealed positions. The two brothers started toward the trees, but paused as they realized they needed to be careful not to reveal their friends' location. Andros scanned the surrounding area for any sign or sound of company, and Ashtar slowly and cautiously made his way toward the men.

After both brothers were at speaking distance, Dalleo spoke out to them.

"Look, there is not much time to explain everything, so I will just tell you what you need to know."

"About the men?" asked Andros in an angry tone.

"No, it has to do with Blakely." At this both brothers drew a little closer. "There are some hard to understand truths that we have discovered. These truths have something to do with you."

Dalleo tried to explain, as clearly as possible, the truth about who Blakely was, where he was from, and the journey the two men were chosen to make. Both men, taken aback by this revelation, began to ask a multitude of questions.

"It may be difficult to understand, but you will just have to trust what Blakely has presented us and follow. We do not have the comfort of time."

"We leave tonight?!" exclaimed Ashtar.

"Yes, we leave now," Dalleo said, frustrated at the brothers' inability to accept his words.

"Boys," Essiah began after this exchange. "Blakely listed your names because he believed you to be honest and true. You do not have to completely understand what and where you are being called to; you just have to trust and follow."

Humbled by the force and wisdom of Essiah, Ashtar said, "Alright, we understand."

"Where are we to go now?" Andros asked.

"At this point, we will all go back and gather Sharai and Perssa." Essiah said.

"Father, what of Blakely's ashes? Where are they?" Dalleo asked.

"They are still with Horrico," Essiah responded. "He told me, not too long ago, that the method for burning the body had worked and that he would keep the ashes until we had figured out how to respectfully scatter them. In all the confusion, they became an afterthought. I suppose I will go speak with Horrico and retrieve them. You go on, and I will meet you at Blakely's home."

"Be careful as you go, father," Dalleo said.

The smirk and grunt that Dalleo received from his father reminded him that his father was well aware of his responsibilities. Dalleo and the brothers retreated back through the trees toward Blakely's home.

No longer trying to make his way undetected, Essiah took the most direct trail to the home of

Horrico. Still, Essiah scanned the forest, not wanting any unnecessary delays or questions. Fortunately, the cold had forced everyone inside, save the raucous men, still hollering in the distant wood. Essiah approached the front grounds and called out to Horrico. Moments later, his old friend appeared, wrapped up in heavy skins and with a confused look on his face.

"Sorry to trouble you, friend. But I have need for Blakely's ashes."

"At this hour? What are you planning on doing with them?"

"I know it sounds strange, Horrico. But unfortunately, I am in a slight hurry and cannot explain."

The trust between these two men was so staunch after all the years together that Horrico needed no more explanation and fetched the ashes from his home. A few moments later, he came out with a clay container and handed it to Essiah with a slight look of concern.

"Do not worry," Essiah said, retrieving the container from Horrico. "I will honor Blakely."

"I know you will," Horrico replied, not knowing Essiah's plans, yet understanding all the same. The two close friends shared a kind look for a moment, and then Essiah rushed away toward Blakely's home.

Meanwhile, Dalleo, Andros, and Ashtar had reached Blakely's home and were now preparing Sharai and the baby for the cold night. Sharai was bundled up in several large cloths and had a large deerskin wrapped tightly around her. Even completely bundled up and with a cloth covering most of her head, Sharai still had a stunning appearance. After consistent crying all day, the baby, Blake, was now sleeping in the powerful arms of his father.

"It is difficult to understand that this very night we are leaving the wood and our people, our families," Sharai remarked.

"These Spaniards are not making it any easier," added Andros after one more loud eruption emanated from outside.

"All this focus on where we are going seems to overshadow the fact that we are leaving all of this, all of them," Dalleo said, looking out at the wood.

"Yes," began Sharai. "But what was that silly little rhyme Blakely would sing? *'Do not hold too tight to your comfort and thrill...*"

"*Lest you be blind to greater things still,*" joined in the others with a good laugh and warm smiles.

Dalleo wrapped Blake up in heavy cloths and a small skin from a coyote. He held him in his arms in such a way that only his small scrunched face peeked through the cloth as he lay asleep in his father's arms. The dark eyes of Dalleo turned misty and soft as he stared lovingly at his son. As he watched the baby spatter and squirm, with each breath he felt as if he was growing closer and closer to his little boy.

With everyone all bundled up and prepared, they all sat along the floor next to Sharai, who still lie on the cloths. Their silent contemplation of all that they might encounter distracted them from noticing Essiah's entrance through the front grounds. Andros noticed him first and greeted him with a firm embrace. As he noticed the clay container in Essiah's hands, the look on his face turned solemn, and he stepped aside to allow Essiah to enter the home.

"If we are to leave," Essiah said, gaining everyone's attention, "the time is now. Mediche and his men have quieted down, and we must take advantage of this."

A hesitation went throughout the room as the reality of their coming journey struck them all. Sharai and Dalleo were the first to arise. Perssa followed, jumping up to assist Sharai.

"This is it," said Ashtar with a sort of nervous excitement. "This has been the last few moments we will spend in this wood."

"I wish we could just be able to say goodbye," Sharai added.

"There is most definitely one person who should be here, whom we are all in great debt to: young Jeran," Dalleo said.

"Poor boy," said Perssa. "He is out there on his own somewhere in the cold."

"Jeran is a wise young man, one of the wisest and most courageous in the wood. He will be fine," Essiah said, making clear with the movements of his body that it was now time to leave.

With several more expressions of confusion and proclamations of disbelief, the group left the home and headed out onto the front grounds. The snow was now coming down heavily and the wind was blowing harshly, so the travelers bundled up even more tightly. Dalleo clutched Blake close to his chest inside the bearskin draped over his shoulders. Sharai stumbled along slowly ahead of them, constantly looking back to make sure all was well. Perssa walked alongside

Sharai as she guided her and reassured her that all would be well and that this night was a great one for her and her family. Finally, Essiah, Ashtar and Andros led the way as they constantly scanned the forest for any sign of movement or any company.

Even as each person in the group knew the way to the Jessap Waters by heart, the blinding snow and frozen ground made the trek difficult and a little unnerving. They relied on the not-to-distant sound of the fast moving waters to guide them in the general direction.

All of a sudden Essiah held up his hand and crouched down a little, grabbing the hatchet from his belt. Andros and Ashtar silently crept up on either side of him, both already holding their hatchets out in front of them, squinting to see the danger Essiah had sensed. Perssa wrapped her arms over Sharai to protect her. Dalleo held Blake even closer to his chest as he also scanned the surroundings for whom or what may be out there.

Seeing and hearing nothing for some time, Andros glanced at Essiah, who was not looking in any specific direction, but rather straining to listen through the sharp blow of the wind.

Andros stood upright and scanned the surrounding forest one more time. Just as he began to suggest moving on, he was struck to the ground as an all too familiar crack emanated from not too far away. Moaning and groaning in pain, he grabbed his shoulder where he had been hit. Moments later the shouts of a large group of men could be heard roughly a stone's throw away. Fear gripped the travelers as they made a dash for the water, which seemed to be the only possible refuge.

Ashtar rushed over and helped Andros struggle along, constantly encouraging his brother to move faster and faster. As they approached the edge of the water, Essiah grabbed the clay container and prepared to spread its contents over the water. The group soon gathered around him at the icy water's edge, fearing their attackers at their heels and anticipating the mysterious future. Before Essiah could pour the contents into the water, he was startlingly interrupted.

"Do not move one more muscle!" exclaimed Mediche from somewhere close behind them. "You know the weapons we hold and what we are capable of doing to you and the rest of your people!"

Essiah slowly lowered the container, set it on the ground, and turned around to find his enemy. He saw Mediche approaching him, followed closely by Oroso and Don Villa, slowly making their way out of the tree cover. With his hatchet in one hand, Dalleo handed Blake over to Sharai and joined his father, Andros, and Ashtar to form a shield between the women and the rival men. The four of them anxiously stood on the balls of their feet with their hatchets raised high.

"I would lower you weapons," Mediche said in a condescending tone. "You are no match for us."

As Mediche said this, the four men could hear brief shouts of what must have been twenty other Spaniards surrounding them from within the trees.

"Your treachery to this people and to this wood will be paid for!" Essiah exclaimed.

"Oh, too true, señor. I shall be paid with tremendous adoration from the rest of your people back in the wood and with great reward from my own people for acquiring this land and its resources. Oh yes, señor, I will be paid," he said with a malicious growl.

"And what business have you with us now?" asked Andros, struggling through the pain in his shoulder. "Why do you follow us and attack without warning?"

"You are fools," shouted Don Villa, stepping forward so that all could see him clearly. "Your behavior and ridiculous actions have caused instability among some of your people. No one knows what you are up to tonight, but your secrets and sneaking tell me I would benefit in stopping you. Still, your disappearance, although unfortunate, would allow me to finally teach your people that we are their only hope for survival. They would seek our guidance in this horrible and tragic time, and we will teach them of the fortune they could have if they come along with us."

"All of this for your own glory!" Dalleo exclaimed in a fury that was in danger of erupting into action.

"How little you understand of us, señor," Mediche said in a mockingly calm tone. "This is not for our glory. It is for the glory of your people, that they might join us and become forefathers of civilizing such an... uncivilized world."

"You may believe that your men will be able to kill us in the end. But that will not be before I have my way with you!" Dalleo exclaimed with a ferocity that frightened Mediche, even in his arrogance, enough to hastily shout out the command to attack.

The command was followed only by the sound of his voice echoing off the surrounding trees and rocks. Mediche turned his head slightly and shouted out his order once more. After a few moments of confusion, Don Villa erupted with his own order. Not a sound came from the forest with the exception of the wind blowing through the trees.

Dalleo and the other travelers could see Mediche and Don Villa becoming more and more vulnerable, but they restrained from attacking as they waited for the moment to reveal itself. They received an immediate answer; a small, yet sturdy, voice came through the forest.

"Go! Do not hesitate, Dalleo! Go!" came the much welcomed voice of Jeran from somewhere within the trees.

"Follow as you have been called," came Dilen's voice from another location.

"Have no fear, father. We will do what we can to restore the wood," followed the voice of Drake from another position still.

Not completely understanding what had just occurred, Essiah led the others to the water's edge once more. Ignoring the shouts and curses from the three Spaniards behind them, who were apparently now involved in some struggle, Essiah reached for the clay container and held it out in front of him.

"I know we are frightened," he began. "Much of this does not make sense and does not seem real. Yet we have been chosen to follow, and follow we must. We must, at this time, not rely upon our own understanding, but trust in Blakely's guidance, which has never led us astray. With that trust, we must follow. I will empty his ashes into the water, and it is then we must jump. Fear not the water! Fear not the cold! Blakely has brought us to this moment, and we must follow one more step!"

The look in Sharai's eyes as she stared at the freezing and treacherous water was one of utter despair and panic.

Dalleo noticed this and said to her, "I will jump first to assure you that wherever it is that I end up, I will be waiting for you and our son."

With these last words, Dalleo turned to his father and nodded for him to proceed. Essiah turned the container over as Ashtar and Andros prepared to jump. The ashes flowed from the container. Some of it was caught by the wind and blown into the air while the rest found its way to the water.

Suddenly, a great fog and a strong wind swirled around Essiah as he yelled to Perssa, Dalleo and Sharai; Ashtar and Andros had just jumped and vanished into the fog. Dalleo watched as Perssa took a quick step forward into the fog and then was gone. Before he could to take one step more, Sharai grabbed his hand and stepped up with him.

"We go together!" she yelled through the noise.

With that, all four of them, Dalleo, Sharai, Blake, and Essiah, stepped into the fog, and Essiah dropped the container into the water. The fog and wind made one last loud clap before the wood was left with only the sound of a calm breeze.

Jeran slowly walked out to the water's edge. With a tear in his eye, he stood there in silence and looked upon the rushing waters.

Presently he was joined by Dilen and Drake as they also paused staring at the water.

"They are where they have been called to be," Jeran said after a few moments.

"And that means that you too, young... I mean Jeran, are to follow as you have been called," Drake said, putting his arm around Jeran.

"Jessap left you in charge of this wood. You are the connection between them and us. What will be your first command?" Dilen said with a smile.

"The men have all been taken care of?" Jeran asked.

"Completely tied up," said Drake.

"Not by your knots I hope," said Dilen, "or they would be free by now."

A soft laughter went up from the three men standing there, and Jeran took one final look at the rushing water.

"I must meet with Horrico in the morning. We must find a way to make fire," Jeran said.

"Why is that?" asked Dilen.

"Well, tomorrow there will be no moon," he replied, turning to the brothers. "How else are we going to have a story telling night without the fire?"

As the three of them had turned to head back to the wood, Jeran reached down and picked up a smooth rock at his feet. Heading back to the wood, he held this stone in his hand, constantly rubbing it as he would for the rest of his life. The people of the wood would always joke that if Jeran was not helping out with repairs, learning to track and hunt, or telling his stories at the fire pit, he could always be found at the Jessap Waters rubbing this stone.

At this end, my grandfather leaned back upon a rock and stared out at the rushing water as it passed our rocky bank. He had finished telling me the tale of what he called *The Legend of the Wood*. He had brought me to this place, he said, because it held some great significance in his story. To me, it was as beautiful as any place I had ever been. The sounds and the smells of the rapid water refreshed every ounce of me. The cry of the eagle and the rhythm of the pecker resounded like a great symphony. The tall pines and aspens surrounding us brought a feeling and the effect of our own private, natural theater. This place, roughly a half-day's hike from my grandfather's land, was his place of refuge and worship every Sunday. As its worth to him was so apparent, it thus beheld great significance to me.

Still in awe of the wonders of this tale, I could have conversed for a lifetime about the heroism of Blakely, the wickedness of Mediche, and the lessons learned through the courage and faith of Jeran. I believed these tales to be some of the best I had ever experienced and always would dig and pine at my Grandfather for more tales from that wood.

Sadly, it was on this day my grandfather told me that the tale of the wood had come to its end. Their lives and experiences as he had known them had all been passed on. Yet it was at this end when he came a little closer with more determination and excitement than I had yet seen. My grandfather grabbed me firmly by the arm and looked passionately into my eyes.

"But that is only the end as I have come to know. That is not the end completely!" he exclaimed.

"What does that mean? How can we find more?" I said, a little startled at the excitement of the old man.

"You must seek for yourself. For just as my grandfather sat on this bank revealing the legend to me and leaving me yearning for more, I leave you yearning for more. Indeed, as is the truth in all of life, if you truly seek something, you will surely find it. And I sought after more of this tale as if I were seeking after water to cure my thirst."

"But how can you find more of a story that is not... well..."

"Real?!" the old man cried, shocked at my question. "Do you mean to tell me you have thought this all some old man's folly? My son, I would have thought better of your heart and logic."

Embarrassed, my head lowered and I felt the great weight of my grandfather's disappointment. That was until he lifted up my chin and told me this, "I will give you proof. But it is exactly that need for proof that makes the legend so invaluable. I know your heart and your mind. I know that you, like Jeran, may need a little help. Let this erase any doubt."

With that, my grandfather arose and slowly retreated toward the spot where we had left our packs. He came back a moment later with his cane, which was all too familiar to me. He placed it at my feet and sat down with a deep sigh. I looked at him in a peculiar way, not completely understanding his intentions. His eyes directed that I look down toward his cane, and I obliged. At first it appeared to be the same cane I had seen my Grandfather carry for as far back as my memory would take me. Yet upon a closer look, I noticed some aged etchings that appeared very faded, yet not completely gone. The etchings were strange and remarkable in their precision. And then it hit me as obvious as anything had ever been. This was *his* cane! Blakely's cane! I could now relate with Dalleo and Jeran upon their great discovery of this remarkable cane. This was indeed the true cane I had come to know through my grandfather's words.

"But how did you…?" I said, stammering over my words at the weight of this discovery.

"I sought, my son," he replied. "I sought."

Made in the USA
Lexington, KY
25 November 2009